"I—I Haven't Given You A Thought Since The Last Time I Saw You," Alexa Said.

Ryan's eyes locked with hers. "I don't believe you."

"What?" A hot flush slowly suffused her cheeks.

"I said I don't believe you. You've thought about me these past two years."

"I heard what you said," Alexa snapped, regaining her composure somewhat. *Somewhat.* "I just couldn't believe you said it, that you're so incredibly vain that you think I've been carrying some stupid torch for you all this time."

"I didn't say you were. But I know you've thought of me."

Oh, she had. Far too often. But she'd rather be struck by lightning than admit it. She opened her mouth to deny ever having had a single thought about him, but he touched her lips with his fingertips.

"I know, because I've thought of you, Alexa," he said quietly. "Too many times..."

Dear Reader:

We have a very special treat for you this month, and we're calling it *Spring Fever*! Here at Desire, we're planning on sending your temperatures rocketing skywards with six sensuous stories written by six spectacular authors.

Just take a look at this fabulous line-up: a *Man of the Month* from Lass Small; the next instalment in the SOMETHING WILD series by Ann Major; and fantastic stories by Dixie Browning, Barbara Boswell, Mary Lynn Baxter and Robin Elliott. And I'm sure you've already noticed that this is one of our now-famous MONTHS OF MEN, with six sinfully sexy hero portraits on the front covers. (Aren't these guys wonderful?)

Enjoy yourselves as Desire gets hot, hot, hot!

Jane Nicholls
Silhouette Books
PO Box 236
Thornton Road
Croydon
Surrey
CR9 3RU

BARBARA BOSWELL
THE BEST REVENGE

Silhouette Desire

Originally Published by Silhouette Books
a division of
Harlequin Enterprises Ltd.

DID YOU PURCHASE THIS BOOK WITHOUT A COVER?
If you did, you should be aware it is **stolen property** as it was reported
unsold and destroyed by a retailer. Neither the Author nor the publisher
has received any payment for this book.

All the characters in this book have no existence outside the imagination of
the Author, and have no relation whatsoever to anyone bearing the same
name or names. They are not even distantly inspired by any individual
known or unknown to the Author, and all the incidents are pure invention.

All rights reserved. The text of this publication or any part thereof may
not be reproduced or transmitted in any form or by any means, electronic
or mechanical, including photocopying, recording, storage in an information retrieval system, or otherwise, without the written permission of
the publisher.

This book is sold subject to the condition that it shall not, by way of trade or
otherwise, be lent, resold, hired out or otherwise circulated without the
prior consent of the publisher in any form of binding or cover other than
that in which it is published and without a similar condition including this
condition being imposed on the subsequent purchaser.

First published in Great Britain in 1994
by Silhouette Books, Eton House, 18-24 Paradise Road,
Richmond, Surrey TW9 1SR

© Barbara Boswell 1993

Silhouette, Silhouette Desire and Colophon are
Trade Marks of Harlequin Enterprises B.V.

ISBN 0 373 59175 6

22-9404

Made and printed in Great Britain

BARBARA BOSWELL

loves writing about families. "I guess family has been a big influence on my writing," she says. "I particularly enjoy writing about how my characters' family relationships affect them."

When Barbara isn't writing or reading, she's spending time with her *own* family—her husband, three daughters and three cats, whom she concedes are the true bosses of their home! She has lived in Europe, but now makes her home in Pennsylvania. She collects miniatures and holiday ornaments, tries to avoid exercise and has somehow found the time to write eight romances for the Silhouette Desire line.

Other Silhouette Books by Barbara Boswell

Silhouette Desire

Rule Breaker
Another Whirlwind Courtship
The Bridal Price
The Baby Track
License To Love
Double Trouble
Triple Treat

One

"Hey, sis, I'm glad you're still here! I was hoping to catch you before you left for the day!" Ben Shaw strode into his sister Alexa's small office, grinning broadly, his blue eyes glowing with purpose.

Alexa glanced up from her paperwork and smiled back. "Hello, Ben."

He bounded around Alexa's desk and grabbed her hands, pulling her to her feet, then enfolding her in a cheerful bear hug.

"You look great, Alexa!" Ben stepped back to gaze raptly at her, still holding her hands. "Wow! Did I say great? What I mean is *gorgeous!* On the Official Ben Shaw Scale of Beauty, which ranges from a frightening minus one to a breathtaking ten, you're a...twelve!"

"Off the scale, hmm?" Alexa stared impassively at her brother. Ben's exuberantly boyish charm and enthusiasm were effective tools that he used to his own advantage, but his sister was quite immune.

"Ben, before you even ask, my answer is no." She withdrew her hands from his and sat back down in her chair. "Whatever you're up to, count me out."

"You're so suspicious!" Ben accused, the brightness of his smile dimming somewhat. "Can't I just drop by to visit? Can't I tell my own sister she's gorgeous, without her assuming that I have some ulterior motive?" He actually managed to sound aggrieved.

But his guilt-inducing tactics fell flat. Alexa was unmoved. "I recognize that unholy gleam in your eye, Benjamin Shaw. And I also know that if I go along with whatever scheme you've cooked up, I'll end up regretting it."

"*Scheme?*" Ben howled indignantly. "I don't have a scheme. I do have a *plan* though, and it's a very good plan that—"

"The answer is no to your plan, too," Alexa cut in. She glanced at her watch. "But while we're on the subject of plans, do you have any for dinner tonight? I have a chicken enchilada casserole in the fridge and I rented the newest Van Damme video to watch on my VCR. Care to join me?"

"I don't wait around for movies to come out on video, I see them when they're first run at the theaters." Ben frowned his disapproval at his sister's life-style. "And yes, I do have plans for dinner tonight—plans that include you. This friend of mine, a really great guy who's seen your picture at my place and practically begged me for an introduction, is—"

"You know how I feel about blind dates, Ben."

"Alexa, this is a guy you should get to know. So I made reservations for—"

"Well, I can't make it." Alexa shrugged. "Sorry," she added as an afterthought.

"You're not the least bit sorry," Ben countered. He heaved a frustrated sigh. "Jeez, Alexa, you're in a rut so deep that—"

"Skip the lecture, Ben. I've heard it from you and Mom and Dad and Carrie and Tyler so often that I can quote every word. Consider it already said."

"It's all Cassidy's fault!" Ben burst out, his face suddenly transformed into a mask of rage. "It always comes back to Ryan Cassidy. Damn him for what he did to you, Alexa." Ben looked older, meaner, brimming with hostility. Quite different from the amiable charmer who had swept so breezily into the office just minutes before.

Alexa knew that few had seen what she called Ben's "rabid dog side." But it took only the slightest allusion, the most vague reference to her erstwhile lover, Ryan Cassidy, to have Ben figuratively frothing at the mouth. Sometimes, it didn't even take that.

Frowning, she ran a hand through the thick tangle of her long blond curls. "Ben, that was a long time ago and I—"

"Yeah, a long time ago and you still haven't recovered!" snapped Ben. "It's been two years since that arrogant, soulless, heartless user did a number on you that caused you to distrust—"

"Ben, let's just drop the subject," Alexa said wearily. She wasn't up to coping with his unmitigated brotherly fury. It took too much energy that she didn't have at the end of a long workday. "It just isn't worth talking about, especially considering the fact that I have no feelings whatsoever for Ryan Cassidy. Not anymore."

"I wish I believed that, Alexa. But Cassidy broke your heart!"

Alexa didn't deny it. "Broken hearts mend, Ben. And mine has." There was no more anger or pain and certainly not a lingering trace of unrequited love for the man she had once hoped to spend the rest of her life with. Unfortunately Ryan Cassidy had declined to mention that he didn't share her dreams of everlasting love; not until the end did he let her know she was nothing more than a temporary, convenient fling.

But that was over and done with. She had faced the painful truth and coped with her broken heart and lost dreams. No, Alexa assured herself, she felt absolutely nothing for Ryan Cassidy anymore.

Ben, however, was a different story. His hatred of Cassidy was pure, unrelenting and completely untainted by time. "He changed you, Alexa." Ben's lips were tight, his eyes narrowed and glittering with emotion. "I saw it happen and it still kills me. You haven't been the same since you fell into the trap that no-good snake laid for you."

"That's ridiculous, Ben," Alexa said impatiently. "You've endowed Ryan Cassidy with entirely too much power. Why, it's reaching mythical proportions! Even worse, you make it sound like I'm some weak, sniveling Victorian maiden who's fallen into a hopeless decline because she's been spurned by the villain of the piece. It's insulting, Ben."

"Cassidy's a villain, all right," Ben agreed darkly. "And you were his innocent victim, Alexa!"

"I was a fool," Alexa amended. "You don't have to remind me of that." She stifled a groan, reluctantly remembering just how much of a fool she'd been. "But it's over and it's been over for a long time, Ben. Give me a little credit, please! I'm in total control of my life and I'm living it exactly the way I want. Professionally I've never been happier. Thanks to Carrie and Tyler, I have my own business, which has always a dream of mine and—"

The door of the office swung open, interrupting her. Alexa jumped to her feet. "Dr. Ellender, hello!" she exclaimed, already walking to greet the tall, graying woman. The hospital was across the lot from the professional building that housed Alexa's office and the facilities she shared with several other physical therapists.

"I have a case that I'd like you to take, Alexa." Dr. Judith Ellender did not believe in wasting time on small talk. Nor would she come to Alexa's office to discuss a case unless she deemed it urgent or important enough to supercede her usual referral by telephone.

Alexa understood the implications of the doctor's personal appearance. "Please sit down, Dr. Ellender," she invited, motioning to the comfortable easy chair placed strategically alongside her desk.

Ben cleared his throat, demanding recognition. Alexa introduced her brother to the Washington area's premier pediatric orthopedic surgeon.

"It's such a pleasure to meet you, Doctor!" Ben exclaimed exuberantly. "Alexa has raved about you so often that I feel as if I already know you!"

Ben's thousand-megawatt smile conveyed the impression that this meeting was the highlight of his life. His blue eyes glowed with such warmth and admiration that even the normally reserved and taciturn Dr. Ellender unbent enough to indulge in a short chat about the excessive rain the D.C. area had been experiencing recently.

Alexa had to admire her brother's conversational style, though she'd been watching him perfect it all their lives.

"Did you know that Alexa and I are triplets?" Ben asked Doctor Ellender ingenuously. The older woman expressed genuine surprise at the fact. Alexa hid a smile. She'd known the doctor for five years and had never exchanged the amount of personal information that Ben had revealed within two minutes.

"Yeah, the three of us—Alexa, me and our sister Carrie—were born twenty-seven years ago on April Fool's Day. Alexa and I are single but Carrie is married," Ben continued expansively. It would never occur to him that this biographical data could be anything but fascinating to his listener. "Her husband is Tyler *Tremaine*." He said the name reverently, like a benediction.

"Ben!" Alexa groaned, flushing. His unadulterated worship of their brother-in-law was downright embarrassing.

"You know, the Tremaine drugstore chain and the Tremaine bookstore chain, two of the fastest-growing, most profitable retailers in the country," Ben elaborated proudly. "The Tremaine wing in the Hospital Center. *Those* Tremaines. Carrie's husband is in line to become president of the entire company. The oldest Tremaine brother will be chairman of the board when their father retires."

Dr. Ellender's lips twitched. "Your—loyalty to your sister's in-laws is commendable," she said dryly.

Alexa was grateful for the doctor's heretofore unrevealed sense of humor. She just as easily could have taken offense at Ben's inexcusable boasting. Nevertheless, it was definitely time to send her brother on his way. Alexa took Ben's arm and forcibly propelled him out the door. "We can't take up any more of Dr. Ellender's time, Ben. Thanks for dropping by."

"Alexa, about tonight," Ben tried one more time.

"Sorry, Ben. The answer's still no." Alexa closed the door firmly behind her.

"Your brother is a charming young man," Dr. Ellender said. "Triplets. How very interesting. Nor did I realize that you were connected to the Tremaine family."

She seemed to be regarding Alexa in a different light, something that invariably happened when people found out that her sister had married into one of the area's richest families. The distinction tended to put Alexa on guard, while Ben positively reveled in it.

"Tyler Tremaine, my brother-in-law, made it possible for me to open my own practice, specializing solely in physical therapy for children," Alexa admitted. "I'd always wanted to, but I couldn't finance it myself. Then Tyler insisted that I—"

"My dear, you needn't explain how you happened to open your own practice, I'm delighted that you did. I always thought you had a special gift for working with children. That's why I continually referred my patients to you. It was annoying when you were employed by the hospital's physical therapy department and couldn't pick and choose your own patients. Many times, certain patients I wanted you to work with were assigned to some other therapist. Since you've been in private practice this past year, that hasn't been a problem. I'm delighted that you can accept all my referrals. Most important, you're not limited to giving therapy in the hospital, you can go into the patients' homes to work with them after discharge. Which brings me to the reason I'm here today...."

Dr. Ellender handed a thick file to Alexa, which she placed on the desktop to be reviewed later. She sat attentively as the doctor launched into the case history. "The patient is a nine-year-old girl who was thrown from a motorcycle when it skidded on some gravel two and a half months ago. August fourth was the exact date of the accident."

Alexa winced, visualizing the accident, a small girl careening through the air and being injured badly enough to require Dr. Ellender's services. And her own.

"Was she wearing a helmet?" Alexa asked quietly. Several of her young patients had suffered falls from bicycles and the like and had not had the protection of headgear. The results were uniformly tragic.

"Yes, she did have on a helmet and mercifully did not sustain any head injuries or brain damage," Dr. Ellender said. But before Alexa could breathe her sigh of relief, the doctor's next words made her breath catch in her throat.

"Unfortunately the child suffered a spinal cord injury in addition to numerous broken bones."

Alexa gripped her pen so tightly that her knuckles turned white. "Paralysis?"

Dr. Ellender nodded grimly. "At first we couldn't ascertain the full extent because of her broken pelvis, but it seems that the child is paralyzed from the knees down. Her hips and thighs are very stiff from being in traction and casted, but she does have sensation and with vigorous physical therapy, hopefully, eventually, will be able to move them normally. ''

"Is the paralysis in her knees and below permanent?" Alexa asked softly.

"We're still uncertain about that at this point. The spinal cord wasn't severed, so the chance for recovery is there, but the nerves were compressed and function is not returning as quickly as we'd hoped. It could be months before we know the full extent of the damage and range of dysfunction. This little girl needs immediate intensive therapy, Alexa. And I don't have to tell you that there are extensive emotional ramifications as well as the obvious physical ones."

"Yes," Alexa said, imagining the distraught parents, the little girl's pain and fear and confusion. And, of course, the terrible consuming anger, both rational and irrational, that was an integral part of such a devastating accident.

"I sincerely hope you will accept this patient, Alexa," Dr. Ellender said earnestly. "You are my first choice of physical therapist for this child. But before you sign on, I think it's only fair to warn you that the family situation in this case is . . . uncertain. Unstable." The doctor paused, rubbed her temples with her fingers, and sighed heavily. "Oh, why bother with euphemisms? It's a calamitous mess, Alexa."

Alexa stared in surprise. Forceful, positive Dr. Judith Ellender rarely sounded so pessimistic.

"How bad?" Alexa asked curiously.

"The parents have been divorced since the patient—her name is Kelsey—was an infant. The mother had custody, though the father supported the child and always remained involved with her. He is extremely bitter toward his ex-wife whom he blames for the accident, and has now decided to gain custody of the child himself."

"So in addition to all the trauma and pain this child has suffered, she's now about to become the object of a custody fight?" Alexa's lips tightened in anger, concern for the injured child rivaling her disgust for the embattled parents. "It just doesn't seem fair, Dr. Ellender."

"Amen to that." Dr. Ellender agreed, rising to her feet. "Kelsey is currently staying with her father. She was released from the hospital to him last week because he has the larger home and has already installed a number of facilities to make it easier to care for the child." The doctor flashed a warm, sudden smile. "Now there's a bright spot—that wonderful, concerned father. He's calm and patient and so eminently reasonable. It's a pleasure to deal with a man like him. I wish all the parents of all my patients could be like him."

"I guess you're going to testify on his behalf during the custody trial," Alexa said wryly.

Dr. Ellender shifted uneasily. "I do have . . . certain reservations about the mother. She's been very difficult with the staff, hysterical and accusatory and, well, so very different from the father. But we needn't go into that matter now, Alexa. I'd like to know if you'll add Kelsey to your caseload, and if you can begin to work with her immediately. Tomorrow isn't a moment too soon. This is a little girl who really needs you."

There was really no decision to make. At least half of her referrals came from the doctor's large pediatric orthopedic practice. Dr. Ellender had mentored Alexa since she first began working at the Hospital Center five years ago, a new graduate armed with her degree in physical therapy. And she owed a good deal of the success of her new private practice to Dr. Ellender's continual referrals and excellent word-of-mouth reviews. She was not about to turn down this personal request.

But there was much more at stake here than that somewhat self-serving reason. There was a little girl who'd been grievously injured and was now facing a terrible emotional crisis. Alexa's abiding love of children couldn't allow her to refuse this patient, no matter who had referred her.

"Of course I'll work with Kelsey, Dr. Ellender," Alexa said. "I'll call her home and schedule an appointment for tomorrow."

Dr. Ellender smiled her approval. "The telephone number is unlisted, but I've written it down on the card attached to the records." She took Alexa's hand in hers, more for a squeeze of encouragement than a formal handshake. "Good luck, Alexa."

"With that landmine family situation you've described, it sounds like both Kelsey and I are going to need it."

"*You're* just what that little girl needs, Alexa. And I do think you will enjoy getting to know Kelsey's father. He has a marvelous sense of humor. A genuine sense of the absurd, which we in medicine can certainly appreciate."

Alexa murmured her agreement. She was half curious and half amused by the doctor's glowing description of the man. Little Kelsey's father certainly had captivated Dr. Ellender, who was rarely enchanted by anyone beyond the childhood years.

"Oh, and he's something of a celebrity, Alexa," Dr. Ellender raved on. "He's a cartoonist, an extremely popular one. You've probably heard of him. I know that I never miss his comic strip in the *Post* every day, and I also own every single one of his books. He was gracious enough to give me an autographed copy of his latest one, which hasn't even been released yet."

Dr. Ellender was positively beaming. "His name is Ryan Cassidy."

The skies were gray and it was drizzling intermittent rain as Alexa parked her car several yards from the front of Ryan Cassidy's house. The grandiose size of the structure discouraged her from pulling right in front and hopping out; one felt obliged to keep that majestic entrance free of vehicles.

A genuine sense of the absurd. Dr. Ellender's words echoed in her ears as Alexa walked up the terraced steps leading to the wraparound porch gracing the front of the house.

She acknowledged the absurdity that she—of all the physical therapists in the entire metropolitan D.C. area, including the outlying sprawling suburbs of Maryland and Virginia—*she* had been the one assigned to this case. But Alexa found no humor in the cosmic joke being played on her.

She hadn't even known that Ryan Cassidy had a child! She'd been in love with him, more deeply involved with him than with any other man in her entire life. She'd wanted to marry him, but he'd neglected to mention the fact that he was a father.

Alexa grimaced. It was a love story with an absurd twist and an unhappy ending—one that could've come right out of one of Ryan's own darkly cynical comic strips.

She hadn't seen Ryan Cassidy for two years, not since the breakup of their intense eight-month relationship. The fact that their paths had not crossed once in all that time was not an accident. She deliberately avoided the places she knew he patronized; in fact, any place he had ever taken her had become off-limits in her quest to steer clear of him. The Washington, D.C., area was large enough for her to be able to easily pull it off.

She purposely didn't read his controversial but ever-popular syndicated comic strip, and she didn't buy the collections of his strips that were issued twice-yearly as paperback books and inevitably made the bestseller lists. The book sales and syndication deal had made him rich enough to own a big house like this, with its long private driveway and elegantly landscaped grounds.

Alexa rapped the brass knocker on the imposingly large door. While waiting to be admitted inside, she cast a cursory glance around her. The house looked like one of those gracious antebellum southern mansions, but she knew from Dr. Ellender, who was downright loquacious on the subject of Ryan Cassidy, that the place was brand-new, completed within the past year. Obviously Cassidy had decided to sink some of his earnings into an abode he deigned fitting for himself. The result was this pretentious suburban copy of a long-gone era, imposing tall white pillars included.

She half expected the door to be opened by an obsequious uniformed servant, in keeping with the theme of the place. Instead Ryan Cassidy himself stood before her, wearing jeans and a dark T-shirt, the same type of attire he'd worn while living in his unpretentious town-house condo back when she'd known him.

Alexa caught her breath. He looked the same as he had back then too, his sandy brown hair, straight and thick and longish, the strong features of his face an intriguing combination of masculine planes and angles. There had been a time when she had adoringly contemplated which she loved more—his mouth, sensual and generous, or his eyes, a deep, rich chocolate-brown color, fringed by thick black lashes.

He was six feet tall, tanned and muscular from his long daily runs—that is, if he still took them. Alexa reminded herself that two long years had passed since she'd exchanged a word with Ryan Cassidy. She didn't know his daily regime anymore, was no longer tuned into his likes and dislikes. Nor did she care to know any of them.

Things were altogether different now, starting with the fact that right now *she* had the upper hand here. For she'd been expecting to see Ryan Cassidy today; she'd braced herself for it, bolstering her resolve by focusing on little Kelsey's needs rather than her own. But by the stunned expression on Ryan's face, he'd obviously had no advance warning of her presence. He looked absolutely shocked to see her standing there.

"Alexa!" He blinked, as if expecting her to dematerialize before his very eyes.

"Yes, I'm Alexa Shaw," Alexa said briskly, as if meeting him for the first time. Well, it wasn't exactly her standard greeting to family members of new patients. Normally she introduced herself with a smile that lighted her pale blue eyes and invited its recipient to smile back. Normally her voice was warm and kind, extending friendship and support.

Right now there was not a trace of a smile on her face, and her eyes were as cold as an Arctic ice floe. Her voice was several degrees colder than that.

"I know who you are," Ryan said with a trace of that testy impatience Alexa remembered well. Ryan Cassidy did not suffer fools gladly, nor did he pretend to. Alexa remembered when *she'd* been the fool whose company he had decided not to suffer, and her body grew even stiffer, her lips tighter. The brief flash of pleasure she had felt at Ryan's discomfiture instantly faded.

"I am the physical therapist referred by Dr. Ellender to treat your daughter, Kelsey," Alexa said in frozen tones. "I called yesterday and set up this appointment with a woman named Gloria Martinez who identified herself as Kelsey's nurse. If there is a problem..." She let her voice trail off, daring him to come up with one.

"Gloria told me she'd spoken with the physical therapist and scheduled the appointment for today," Ryan said, more to himself than to Alexa, as if fitting the pieces together. "Dr. Ellender said she was referring us to one of the area's finest physical therapists for children."

"And you can't believe that could be me?" Alexa demanded with icy indignation.

"No, I—I didn't mean to imply anything like that." Ryan ran his hand through his thick hair, looking and sounding harried. It was not a state that Alexa associated with the unfailingly confident, self-possessed Ryan Cassidy she had known. Or *thought* she'd known.

"Please come in," he said, this time looking and sounding distracted and apologetic.

Alexa stepped inside, somewhat distracted herself at this point. She'd never seen Ryan Cassidy—god of cool—so completely *uncool*.

And he kept it up, looking at the ground, the ceiling, anywhere but at Alexa as he rattled on. "Dr. Ellender mentioned that the physical therapist she was referring for Kelsey was in private practice. I knew you worked at the Hospital Center, therefore I wasn't expecting to see you here, but the doctor assured me that you're exceptionally good so I hope you'll overlook my initial surprise and—"

He yammered on while Alexa gazed at him, more than a little awestruck. *Ryan Cassidy was nervous, and she was the one who'd inspired his anxiety!* He was afraid he'd angered her, afraid she'd take offense and walk out. In the past, she had always been the one to play that part. What a role reversal! It was ironic that when he'd been her lover, he had never minded if he hurt or angered her.

But now, when he'd lost that power over her; now when she no longer cared what he said or did, *now* he decided that her feelings mattered and was willing to pander to her.

Of course, he needed her now more than he had ever needed her then, Alexa conceded cynically. He needed her talent and skill to help his child—the child whose existence he hadn't even bothered to mention to her. Back in the bad old days, when she had been confiding all her thoughts, hopes and dreams to him, planning a future with him, he had not seen fit to share the most basic and crucial fact about himself: that he was the father of a little girl named Kelsey.

Kelsey. Alexa's pale blue eyes narrowed thoughtfully. Her new patient-to-be was the only thing that really mattered here, not the fractured love affair between herself and Ryan. "Look, before you advance to groveling, I accept your apology," she said coolly. "I'm assuming that's what this anxiety attack of yours actually is."

"You assume correctly." Ryan paused to breathe, the last of his rapid run-on sentences trailing off. He stopped his pacing, his eyes ceased their frantic darting. "I never meant to denigrate your professional skills, Alexa. Will you stay?

Please! Will you accept Kelsey as your patient?'' He appeared to be holding his breath, awaiting her answer.

Alexa heard the desperate hope in his voice. She remembered all those times she'd dreamed of hearing him beg her to stay with him. How she'd prayed for it.

Right after their breakup, her fantasies had always ended with her saying yes and him sweeping her into his arms for a joyful reconciliation. Later, when her pain had been transformed into the rage of rejection, the imaginary outcome was quite different. She'd wanted revenge then, and the best revenge she could think of was to throw his pleas back in his face and walk out—after tossing off some appropriately devastating remark that would wound him forever, of course.

The circumstances were different now but she could still make that old revenge scenario work. He was pleading with her and she could refuse him. And she strongly suspected that withholding her professional skills would hurt him far worse than withholding her love ever could have.

She glanced at Ryan and saw him watching her intently. Their eyes met and held for a long silent moment.

''Alexa, I know that what went down between us in the past was—'' he paused and swallowed ''—unpleasant.''

''Unpleasant,'' Alexa repeated. She'd felt as if her whole world had collapsed when he'd left her; he merely considered the incident ''unpleasant.'' The dissentient humor of it appealed to her own sense of the ridiculous.

Alexa raised her brows. ''I like the understatement,'' she said dryly. ''You're not noted for it, but you ought to use it more in your comic strip. Usually your satire is about as subtle as a hydrogen bomb.''

Ryan heaved a frustrated sigh. Alexa remembered how quickly frustration followed impatience with him. She'd once thought it a mark of his high intelligence and creativity, but she had long since reconsidered. Ryan Cassidy was spoiled, used to having his own way and becoming irritable when he didn't immediately get it. There was nothing to romanticize about that.

Right now Ryan was both frustrated and impatient, she knew. He would probably like nothing more than to level her with one of his poisoned-tongued barbs—and his aim was always right on target, scoring a direct hit where one was most vulnerable. It was one of the reasons why his cartoons were so reviled by his targets—and were so amusing to readers vicariously reveling in the attacks.

But Ryan launched no verbal weapons at her. "Alexa, Kelsey is an innocent child." He was trying to mask the anger in his tone, trying to sound reasonable.

Alexa picked up on that immediately. Dishonest as ever, she mentally scorned him. Deceptive and manipulating.

His tone grew more urgent. "Alexa, my daughter had nothing to do with what happened between us and for you to punish her for—"

"Nothing happened between us, Ryan," Alexa cut in with a cool little smile. "We dated each other for a while and then we stopped seeing each other." She liked the idea of reducing Cassidy to a footnote in her dating history. "You surely can't believe that I would refuse to treat your daughter on those grounds."

Ryan stared at her, long and hard. So long and so hard that Alexa felt a slow heat begin to suffuse her cheeks. It took considerable willpower for her to hold his gaze, but she did and she was proud of herself.

"If that's all there was to it, no, I wouldn't worry at all about you refusing to work with Kelsey," Ryan said at last. "But we both know that there was much more to it than that."

"Much more to what?" Alexa asked blithely.

"More to us," Ryan blurted out, his dark eyes glittering.

"There was never an *us,* Ryan. There was you and your own personal agenda and there was me. One had nothing to do with the other." She hadn't figured that out until after it was all over, but she wasn't inclined to forget it.

"For God's sakes, Alexa, don't play word games. I know you must feel bitter at the way I—"

"Don't ever presume to know how I feel about anything," Alexa snapped. "When it comes to feelings and normal human behavior, you don't have a clue, which is probably why you're such a successful cartoonist. Your demented characters are so remote from reality that—"

"Reality is far more demented and perverse than anything I've ever come up with," Ryan interrupted darkly.

Alexa saw the pain in his dark brown eyes, she heard it in his jagged tones. She was human enough to wish that she hadn't, because as long as she saw Ryan as her hated adversary, she could fight him, scorn him, keep her emotional distance. But seeing him as a distraught parent, so like all the other parents of her other young patients, totally reversed her perceptions.

His child had been seriously injured, could no longer walk or run or do many of the things that normal, active nine-year-olds do. Alexa had seen the despair on his face mirrored in the faces of so many others and she never failed to respond.

"Kelsey's condition is the only thing that matters here," she said quietly, her light blue eyes wide and serious. "I've studied her medical records and worked up a regime of exercises and treatment for her that have worked well for similar injuries in other patients."

"Will she ever walk again?" Ryan asked raspily.

"Yes," Alexa's reply was immediate and firm.

"I don't mean with braces and crutches or canes. I don't mean taking a few tortured steps at a time while clutching on to a walker," Ryan raged. "Those are some of the options that have been offered to us and I don't want them. I want my little girl to run to meet me, I want to see her ride her bike and roller-skate and jump rope. I want her to be able to show me what she learned in her dance class."

"I wish I could make those promises, but I can't so we won't focus on that. We'll focus on what can be accomplished every day, hour by hour. It takes time and patience but—"

"Time and patience!" Ryan repeated furiously. "Time and patience." This time he mimicked exactly her calm, measured professional tones. "You and your cohorts in the medical field love to toss platitudes around, but none of you is confined to a bed or a wheelchair, none of you has to hear your own child crying because she can't do the things she loves to do. So don't give me the time-and-patience crap, because it's a stall and I'm not buying it."

"You want action, not talk," Alexa said, her voice lowering as his rose.

"Yes, dammit!"

"Then I suggest you shut up and take me to Kelsey so we can get started right away."

Two

———

Alexa followed Ryan up the red-carpeted staircase, her eyes widening at the grandiosity of the place. Had an entire forest been felled to provide the long, tall elaborate wooden banister? She glanced over it to the foyer below. It was the size of her apartment's combined living and dining room! And the chandelier that hung there looked like something out of the palace of Versailles. Before she could control it, a grin stole across her face.

"What's so funny?" demanded Ryan.

She was startled that he'd caught her smirking. He had been walking a few paces ahead of her—his lord of the manor stride?—and she hadn't expected him to be watching her.

"Your house is what's funny," she said frankly. Why secretly mock the place when she could do it openly? "It's the most ostentatious place I've ever seen."

"Are you always this blunt with your new clients?" Ryan asked, equally blunt.

Alexa shook her head. "I'm usually quite tactful. In fact, diplomacy has always been one of my strong suits."

"Well, it seems your tact and diplomatic skills have taken a leave of absence."

"It does seem that way." Alexa nodded thoughtfully, knowing that if he was the parent of any other of her patients, particularly one she was meeting for the first time, she would be behaving quite differently.

"Maybe it's this mansion of yours," she mused. "The insanity of it seems to bring out something irrational in me. I find myself wondering whether you see yourself as Rhett Butler or King Louis? Or maybe a combination of both? Whatever, the decor around here spans the eras—and countries too."

"I definitely won't show you the Japanese garden out back," Ryan said wryly. "You'll accuse me of harboring Emperor Hirohito delusions."

Alexa paused on the stairs, staring oddly at him. "You *know* that this place is—"

"Ridiculous?" Ryan suggested. He stopped two steps ahead of her and leaned against the banister. "Of course I do." He laughed shortly. "How could I not?"

"But according to Dr. Ellender, you had it built. You must've had some say in the—uh—design and decor." She was truly puzzled now. "Were you having a—a mid-life crisis or something and this place is the result?"

"I thought the props of a mid-life crisis were the acquisition of a giggly blonde in Spandex and a hot red sportscar, not a garishly overdone house. *This* is simply bad taste." Ryan grimaced. "Anyway, I just turned thirty-five last month. Isn't that too young to have a mid-life crisis?"

"I don't know. You tell me. Because this place seems so out of character for you. It's like something you'd lampoon in one of your strips."

"Thank you for that, at least. And I happen to agree with you. It's a classic nouveau riche showpiece—aspiring to be high class and elegant when it's actually embarrassingly pretentious and gaudy. Wait until you see the bathrooms. You won't be able to keep a straight face."

"I don't get it," Alexa said flatly, folding her arms and staring up at him. "You ridicule it, but you must've given your okay for all of this."

"I gave the decorator carte blanche," Ryan admitted. "She wasn't shy about making suggestions to the architect, either. Thus the pillars, the grand staircase and the mile-high ceiling in the entrance hall. I never even saw the place until I moved in earlier this year. And when I did, my thoughts ran along the same line as yours—that I was now living in one of my own cartoon settings. Some would say that's a fitting revenge, I guess."

Alexa thought of the heat sparked by his controversial, irreverent and bitingly caustic strips. "No, your targets would think this place is way too good for you. They'd rather see you living in a cave without plumbing or electricity."

"Preferably without food and oxygen, too," Ryan added dryly. "But this place is a punishment in its own right. Have you ever taken a shower with the water spouting out of a gold swan's mouth? At least a cave has a certain dignity."

"I assume the decorator was your girlfriend of the moment? And that the relationship ended as soon as you walked into that astonishing foyer?"

"No, I made it past that. It wasn't until I saw the jungle motif in the master bedroom that she was history."

Ryan grimaced wryly. He was not about to confide that the decorator responsible for this bizarre assault on the senses was Stepmother Number Three, Nadine Cassidy, whom he felt had been treacherously betrayed by her husband, one Ron Cassidy, Ryan's ever-loving dad. To reclaim her life, poor Nadine had decided to go into interior decorating, and Ryan felt he owed it to her to be her first client. After seeing this place, he wondered if he would be her last.

"Jungle motif? The decor even spans the continents!" Alexa almost laughed, but caught herself just in time. It seemed that Ryan had made his decorator girlfriend "history" as swiftly and expediently as he'd expunged her. Whatever their differences in tastes, both she and the hapless decorator were Ryan Cassidy castoffs. Even worse, she was beginning to drop her guard around him, to be sucked in by his self-deprecating humor. She mustn't forget that Cassidy possessed the skills to make himself as likable as he cared to be. But this time she would not be charmed!

Her withdrawal was palpable. Ryan saw her pale blue eyes turn cold, he watched the beginnings of her smile turn instead to a stony frown. *Cut the banter and get moving,* he advised himself. It was time to get back on the therapist-and-parent-of-the-patient track immediately, for both his own and Alexa's sakes. Because simply by spending time with her, he could feel himself being drawn to her, wanting to prolong that time...

He gave himself a swift mental shake. That couldn't be allowed to happen. She was entirely too alluring, and he had already learned that he was particularly susceptible to her appeal. He had tangled emotionally with Alexa Shaw before and extricating himself had been—hard—on them both.

Another understatement, Ryan thought wryly. Maybe he was finally developing a penchant for that subtle art because *hard* was definitely an understated description of the terrible despair that had gripped him two years ago when he and Alexa had gone their separate ways.

He had hurt her badly, and the pain he caused her had ricocheted back to him. He remembered those dark days, the emptiness, the raw aching pain. And he remembered the anger he'd felt, at himself for stupidly and unexpectedly falling in love with her, and at Alexa for making him do it.

Yet knowing all this, recalling it in vivid detail, did not compel him to take the necessary steps—both literally and figuratively—away from her. Instead he stayed where she was, standing two steps above her, staring at her.

She was a pleasure to look at, her features delicate with high cheekbones and a soft, well-shaped mouth. Her eyes were an arresting color of light blue, huge, wide-set and expressive. And her hair, long thick and honey blond, a full mane of natural curls that no perm could ever duplicate, inevitably drew second glances from admiring men and women alike.

She was slender and tall at five-feet-seven, and though her loose-fitting jeans, celery-green T-shirt and long, oyster-colored jacket concealed the curves of her figure, he knew from their past shared experiences that she certainly had them. Rounded full breasts, a narrow waist and gently flaring hips, long shapely legs that he well remembered admiring, touching, feeling wrapped tightly around him . . .

Heat surged through him. He'd been attracted to her from the moment he had first seen her, pumping her own gas in the self-service filling station near the fruit-and-vegetable stand where both had been buying local farm produce that summer. Their paths had never crossed before, though they learned later that they both made weekly trips to the stand.

He'd caught himself staring at Alexa, watching her graceful, efficient movements. She didn't seek anyone's help as she competently filled her car's tank, so they didn't meet cutely over a spewing gasoline hose. She wasn't even aware that he was watching her from the anonymity of the opposite service island.

Ryan hadn't planned to initiate any sort of encounter; he'd had no intentions of pursuing her. But when Alexa had climbed into her car without once glancing in his direction, he had found himself speeding over to rap on her window. Inside was another young blonde, whom he'd later learned was her triplet sister, Carrie. Both young women had looked warily at him, uneasy at being approached by a stranger. He'd had to do some fast smooth talking, make an intense effort to be charming, witty and unthreatening, to keep them from driving away. When he'd succeeded in getting Alexa's name and phone number he had felt as triumphant

as an ambitious high school senior who had just been accepted at Yale. With a full scholarship.

During those following eight months with her, he'd spent
some of the happiest days of his life. There hadn't been
anything or anyone to equal those days since their breakup.

A sharp pang of guilt ripped through him as the memory
of Alexa's face, pale with pain when he'd told her it was all
over between them, flashed unwillingly to mind. She hadn't
deserved to be hurt but he had been too self-absorbed, too
caught up in his own misery to consider hers. And though
he still thought of her at odd hours of the day and night, he
hadn't seen her since they'd parted. Not until today.

"Why are you staring at me ?" Alexa's voice, sharp and
cold, punctured his reverie.

Ryan immediately averted his eyes. "Was I staring?" he
asked. He sounded cool and slightly amused. It was one of
his major talents—a survival skill, really—presenting an
appearance that convincingly belied his true feelings.

"Yes, you were," Alexa said firmly. There had been a
time when she would have questioned her own perceptions,
blushed and apologized for them. Not anymore. "Like a
beady-eyed jackal."

"A jackal? Beady-eyed? " He pondered which was the
more insulting. "Well, anyway, I like the imagery. In fact,
there's a certain politician with a decidedly fascist streak
who could be easily transformed into a beady-eyed jackal
and incorporated in my current storyline. Since I'm already
a month ahead with the strips, watch for him to appear
around Thanksgiving."

"I don't read your work," she said succinctly. "I don't
like it."

"Oh. Well, you're in good company there. I've been told
that the President would rather resign the office than read
one of my strips. I've received hate mail from both houses
of Congress and from a whole score of activist groups. And
that's just politics! One must also factor in my enemies in

the entertainment, business and religious communiti..
quite a sizable list.''

''And that makes you very happy, doesn't it? Having enemies and being hated is far preferable to you than being
loved.''

His eyes met and held hers. ''It's a lot less demanding,''
he said coolly. ''Far less emotional. And since my loved ones
invariably seem to end up as my enemies, I've decided it's
more honest to begin as—''

''You've never had an honest moment in your life,''
Alexa cut in, her voice mirroring the disgust and anger in her
eyes. ''Not an honest thought or an honest emotion. You're
the biggest phony there is.''

''Considering that this is the nation's capital, there is a lot
of competition for that particular title. It's quite a distinction you've bestowed on me. Thank you, I think.'' Grinning, looking as pleased as the Cheshire Cat, he turned and
continued up the stairs.

Alexa had no choice but to follow him. Her choice had
already been made, when she'd agreed to accept Kelsey, Dr.
Ellender's young patient, as her own. She must put her
personal animosity toward little Kelsey's father aside and
concentrate solely on the child.

Ryan opened a set of white double doors leading into the
biggest, brightest bedroom Alexa had ever seen. Her eyes
darted around in astonished wonder at the primary-colored
walls—each one different!—the blinding orange carpet, and
built-in shelves that held as many toys and games as an aisle
at a toy store. An enormous wooden dollhouse, completely
furnished and inhabited by a legion of tiny dolls, domi-
nated one corner of the room and a carousel horse—the real
thing, painted with every color of the rainbow—reigned over
another corner.

The jarring note in this kiddie's fantasy room was the
presence of the hospital bed, complete with a trapeze and
pulleys over the top of it. And in the bed was a little girl,
with blunt-cut, chin-length sandy brown hair and big brown

eyes, the color of dark chocolate. She was wearing a bright yellow sweat suit with a unicorn printed on the shirt.

Alexa sucked in her breath. The child's coloring was the same as Ryan's, her features, though smaller and distinctly feminine, definitely favored him, as well. Near the bed was a child-size wheelchair, further testimony to the unfortunate changes that had taken place in Kelsey Cassidy's young life.

Alexa glanced at Ryan, standing beside her, and saw him tense.

"Kelsey, sweetheart, this is Alexa Shaw the physical therapist who will be working with you." Ryan's voice sounded strained, yet determinedly, overly cheerful. "Say hello to her, Kelse."

Kelsey briefly looked away from the humongous television screen she was watching. "Why'd she have to come in the middle of *All My Children,* Mommy?" Kelsey demanded of the woman sitting in a chair beside the bed.

Alexa's eyes followed Ryan's to the big blue leather recliner to see a petite, dark-eyed young woman with a long, stylishly arranged mane of ink-black hair, rise quickly to her feet. She was very attractive in a sexy, sultry way, her compact figure displayed to perfection by the tight black jeans and snug aqua cotton sweater she wore.

So this was Ryan's ex-wife, the mother of his child? She looked around thirty, give or take a year. And she appeared to be both nervous and defensive as she rose to her feet.

"Why are you still here, Melissa? I thought you said you were leaving after lunch." Ryan's tone was definitely unfriendly, even hostile.

"Well, I didn't, did I?" the woman named Melissa replied, her tone matching Ryan's.

"Be quiet! I'm watching the show!" ordered Kelsey, her glare, her tone of voice, perfectly aping her parents.

"We'll tape the rest of it, honey," Melissa said, pressing some buttons on the remote. Though the television stayed

on, the VCR beneath it clicked into action. "You can __
it later."

"I wanna watch it *now!*" demanded Kelsey.

"A child her age shouldn't be watching soap operas anyway," Ryan asserted, glaring accusingly at Kelsey's mother.
"She should be reading or drawing or—"

"I hate to read and draw," Kelsey informed them all. "I
only like to watch TV and that's all I'm going to do. And I
want *her* to go away." She pointed her finger at Alexa.

Alexa sprang into action. "Sorry, you're stuck with me—
for a while anyway," she said good-naturedly, crossing the
room to stand beside Kelsey's bed. "Hello, Kelsey." Next
she directed her gaze to the woman who was standing on the
other side of the bed, her posture rigid with tension. She
extended her hand. "And you're Kelsey's mother? I'm
pleased to meet you."

The woman stared warily at her, then glanced swiftly at
the unsmiling Ryan who was watching them both with unmistakable disapproval. Apparently this scored some points
in Alexa's favor with the mother for she hesitantly took
Alexa's hand to shake.

Ryan strode across the room to stand at the foot of
Kelsey's bed. "Allow me to make the introductions." A
perfectly innocuous statement but his tone seemed to accuse them both of a criminal conspiracy. "Alexa Shaw, this
is Melissa Mihalic, Kelsey's mother."

"I go by Melissa *Cassidy,* too," Melissa said, shooting a
malicious smile in Ryan's direction. His grim expression
seemed to please her. Obviously she knew that he did not
care for her continued use of his surname. "When you have
a kid, sometimes it's easier to use the same last name at
times, even when you're divorced," Melissa explained
breezily to Alexa.

"I understand," Alexa murmured. She hoped she
sounded sufficiently neutral; she felt like the demilitarized
zone between two warring countries.

"Then why don't you ever use the last name Webber, Mommy? " Kelsey piped up. "You have a kid with that name, too." The little girl turned to Alexa, her brown eyes wide with an unnerving combination of innocence and guile. "I have a little brother named Kyle, but Mommy's not divorced from his father because she never married him." She smiled brightly. "But you don't have to be married to have a baby, you know."

Alexa glanced from Ryan's tight, disapproving face to Melissa's anxious one, then back to Kelsey, who was positively beaming. And no wonder, Alexa mused; this angelic-looking little girl had scored a direct ballistic hit with her seemingly spontaneous chatter. Alexa wasn't fooled for a minute. Little Kelsey's remarks had been carefully calculated to achieve maximum impact.

Ryan's paternal response was immediate. "While it's true a woman can have a baby without being married, I firmly believe that it's best for the baby when its parents *are* married, Kelsey," he said tautly. His dark eyes were glittering with angry disapproval. "I understand that you see other examples, from daytime television and from your own mother's behavior, but I sincerely hope you don't think it's the right thing to do and that you won't imitate them when you're older."

"The right thing to do," Melissa repeated scornfully. "You're such a self-righteous hypocrite, Ryan."

Alexa watched Kelsey glance from one parent to the other, and then back to the TV screen, with a small satisfied smile. One didn't have to be gifted with ESP to know that this was a long-standing source of conflict between Ryan and his ex-wife, and that Kelsey deliberately had set the argument in motion so she could tune back into her television program while the adults kept themselves otherwise occupied.

Alexa felt a kinship with the UN peacekeeping force. "Can we call a cease-fire and work together here?" she volunteered bravely. "I'd like to get Kelsey started today with some passive exercises. Kelsey, I have some portable equipment out in my car. Want to come with me to get it?''

''It's raining,'' both Ryan and Melissa chorused together.

Alexa wondered if it was the first thing they'd both agreed on in years. ''It's only drizzling and there's no thunder or lightning,'' she amended heartily. ''And it's a warm afternoon. A little water isn't going to hurt you, is it, Kelsey? You won't melt. It's not like you're the Wicked Witch of the West or something.''

''She'll catch a cold if she goes out and gets wet,'' cried Melissa.

''This is ridiculous! Of course you can't take a sick child out in the rain,'' Ryan said firmly.

Alexa shrugged. ''Okay, I'll go myself.'' She started toward the door but not before she stole a quick glance at Kelsey. The calculating expression on the child's face spoke volumes. Alexa took a deep breath and waited; Kelsey did not disappoint her.

''I want to go outside!'' the child bellowed. ''I like the rain and I'm not sick!'' She tried to inch herself toward the edge of her bed. ''Get me out of here!'' she demanded. ''I'm going outside.''

Alexa walked back to the bed. ''Grab the trapeze and see how far you can shift yourself over toward the chair, Kelsey,'' she suggested. ''We'll see how strong you are and how much work needs to be done to increase your upper-body strength.''

Kelsey reached up and grabbed the trapeze, but before she could do anything at all, Ryan swooped down and scooped her up in his arms. ''If you want to get into the chair, I'll put you in, sweetheart.'' He did so, settling her in the wheelchair. ''You can go downstairs and out onto the porch because it's covered but—''

''I just looked out the window and she's right, it's only drizzling with no thunder and lightning,'' Melissa cut in. ''I guess there's really no reason why Kelsey can't go out to the car with her. It'll be fun to get out in the rain again, won't it, Kelse? Remember how much fun you used to have splashing in those puddles on the playground?''

"Uh-huh." Kelsey looked up at Alexa. "What's your last name again?''

"Shaw," Alexa said. "My name is Alexa Shaw." She could already tell by the gleam in the child's eye that another strategy was in the works.

"Do you always use Shaw as your last name? All the time?'' Kelsey asked sweetly, and Alexa nodded again, waiting.

The salvo was not long in coming. "Well, I'm like my mom 'cause sometimes I use two different last names,'' Kelsey went on brightly. "Sometimes I'm Kelsey Cassidy and sometimes I'm Kelsey Webber 'cause that's Jack's name. He's Kyle's daddy and he lives with us and he's kinda like my daddy, too. Today, I'm Kelsey Webber,'' she added, as if relishing the sound.

Another bull's-eye. This was not artless childish prattle; Kelsey knew exactly the effect her words would have on her father. Alexa saw the pain flash across Ryan's face before he quickly lowered his eyes.

"C'mon, Alexa, or whatever your name is, we have an elevator,'' Kelsey said cheerfully, pushing the wheels of the chair to propel herself forward. "I'll show you where it is.''

Alexa followed her, leaving the embattled parents behind. "Maybe you really should avoid the rain, Kelsey,'' she said thoughtfully, walking alongside the chair, out of the room and into the spacious hall. "In fact, maybe you should stay completely away from all water. You just might melt, after all.''

"I saw *The Wizard of Oz,* y'know,'' Kelsey said archly. "I know the Wicked Witch of the West melted when she got water on her.''

"Exactly. And I'm beginning to think you might be one of her direct descendants. So I advise taking extra precaution around water.''

"If I told my dad you called me a witch, he'd fire you right away."

"I'm sure he would. And then your mom would decide I'm the best and only physical therapist in the world for you and they'd be back at war again, wouldn't they? I saw the way you set them up, Kelsey. Do you like to see them fight?"

Kelsey shrugged. "Well, when they're fighting, they leave me alone."

"And you can watch TV in peace," Alexa guessed. "Where's this elevator, anyway?"

"Turn here. Daddy had it put in. You know, after the accident."

"I see."

"He wants me to live here with him. He wants—custody—" Kelsey said the word very carefully "—'cause he's mad that I was on Jack's motorcycle and Jack skidded off the road and I fell off and got hurt real bad."

"You were riding with Jack when you fell off?" Alexa considered the implications of that. Ryan's child injured on a motorcycle driven by his ex-wife's lover—and father of her other child. Add to that, the blatant animosity between Ryan and Melissa, and the family situation was all that Dr. Ellender had described.

"Are you mad at Jack for the accident?" Alexa asked bluntly.

Kelsey stopped pushing the wheels and stared up at her in genuine surprise. "No!" she exclaimed at once. "It isn't Jack's fault. It was an accident."

"He must feel terrible about it," Alexa said.

Kelsey nodded vigorously. "I even saw him crying!" she confided. "I couldn't believe it. My mom cries a lot but Jack never cries!"

"What about your dad?" Alexa asked curiously.

"He doesn't cry but he's sad about the accident. He's mad too. *Real mad,*" she repeated, stressing the words.

"There's a lot of anger in this house," Alexa observed.

"Yeah," Kelsey agreed. "Lots of yelling and fighting. There's the elevator," she called, pointing to the structure tucked behind the staircase. "If you like peace and quiet, you shouldn't come here," the little girl added seriously.

Alexa pressed the button and the doors immediately snapped open. She helped Kelsey maneuver the wheelchair into the small elevator car. "I prefer peace and quiet over fighting, but I think you're worth sticking it out for in this war zone, Kelsey. Maybe we can even get the fighting to de-escalate. That's a military term, de-escalate. It means to decrease in volume or scope."

"De-escalate," Kelsey repeated. She folded her arms, and Alexa had to take over pushing the wheelchair from behind. "I don't know. I just don't know."

"Well, think it over, okay?" Alexa wheeled the little girl outside onto the porch, just in time to see the previously light rain turn into a teeming deluge. She heaved a sigh. "Looks like this has turned into a major downpour. We can't go out in it now."

"Why not? Are you afraid *you'll* melt, Wicked Witch?" Kelsey challenged.

"I'm afraid we'll both drown. At the very least we'll get soaked and look like a pair of drowned rats."

A crack of thunder sounded as a sudden flash of lightning streaked the sky. "I guess that takes care of that," Alexa said firmly. "I have to get you back inside before this metal chair acts as a lightning rod and fries you."

Kelsey giggled.

"What a horrible thing to say to a child!" Ryan was behind them and he wasn't laughing.

"It was just a joke, Ryan." Behind him stood Melissa. She looked over at Alexa and then suddenly smiled. "Anyway, Kelsey thought it was funny."

"Oh, the electrocution of a child is downright hilarious," Ryan said sarcastically. "And I certainly do not appreciate a joke about my own child being struck by lightning! Do you think you can possibly understand that?"

He was glaring at Alexa and she knew that this time his biting remonstrance was directed at her rather than Melissa.

So she answered him. "Yes, I understand. But I'd have thought that someone who uses politics and disease and crime—not to mention global and family strife—as topics for his comic strip would find humor in anything." She turned to push Kelsey's chair back inside.

Ryan was beside her in an instant, and Alexa quickly moved aside. There was no physical contact between them but his very nearness sent a queer, pulsing rush through her. Moving even farther away, Alexa watched him take his place behind the wheelchair, his hands gripping the bars.

"I'm afraid this just isn't going to work out," he said tersely, his dark eyes glittering. "I respect Dr. Ellender's judgment, but she is simply going to have to recommend another therapist. I'll see that you are compensated for your time here today, but your services will not be required in the future, Alexa."

Ryan Cassidy was a master at the cold formal dismissal, Alexa acknowledged grimly to herself. And now she'd had the searing experience of being dismissed by him twice— once personally, the second professionally. She took a deep breath, fighting to keep her emotions under control.

"Her services are most definitely required here! " Melissa's voice, high-pitched and strident, broke the tense momentary silence. She moved quickly to stand beside Alexa, placing a possessive arm around her.

Alexa was vaguely aware of the ridiculous picture they must present because her champion, Melissa, was at least six or seven inches shorter.

"I'm not going to let you fire her!" Melissa exclaimed, her dark eyes flashing. "She's the very best therapist that there is for Kelsey, and I insist that she stay."

"It's just like you said, Alexa!" Kelsey blurted out, her brown eyes wide, her tone full of wonder.

Alexa couldn't help but smile. Despite her craftiness, Kelsey was just a nine-year-old, after all. "Well, predicting the future is one of my sidelines," she said lightly. "I prefer using a crystal ball, but palms and tea leaves will do in a pinch."

"Is the crystal ball in your car?" Kelsey asked interestedly.

"She's just kidding, Kelsey," her mother interjected.

Kelsey obviously wasn't certain about that. "What's going to happen now, Alexa?" she pressed.

"*I* can tell you what's going to happen, Kelsey. Alexa is going to be your physical therapist," Melissa said firmly. She glowered at her ex-husband. "She is the first person in the entire medical profession who hasn't sucked up to you since Kelsey's accident, and you can't stand it, can you, Ryan? You want to get rid of her because she treated me like a human being instead of a hysterical, unreasonable—"

"If you've been treated like you're hysterical and unreasonable, it's because you've behaved that way, Melissa," Ryan interrupted coldly.

"My baby was hurt and from the very first day, from the very first hour, I was shunted aside by everybody in that damn hospital because they're so in awe of the great Ryan Cassidy. Mr. Hotshot Comic-strip Artist. Mr. Hip Celebrity Cartoonist!" Melissa's voice rose.

She was starting to sound hysterical, Alexa thought. But unreasonable? Dr. Ellender's admiring description of Ryan sprang to mind—along with her less-than-glowing words about Melissa.

"It's true," Melissa cried, turning to Alexa. "He charmed the entire hospital staff, the doctors and nurses, right down to the dietary aides! He made jokes and drew them little cartoons, he gave them all books of his comic-strip collections. How could I compete with him? He also made it very clear that *he* was the one paying the bills and that *I* was the enemy—a nagging, unpleasant inconvenience to be ignored."

"That is absolutely untrue," Ryan countered angrily. "Whatever negative responses you might have received were brought on entirely by yourself, by your own words and actions, Melissa. Not mine. I was never in competition with you for the hospital staff's favor, I was simply concerned with my child's condition. And I insist that you stop these histrionic, unfounded accusations of yours. They are bound to be upsetting to Kelsey."

Alexa was watching Kelsey who didn't appear to be unduly upset but who was taking in every word, looking from one parent to the other, as if carefully assessing the situation. When her eyes met Alexa's, the child smiled sweetly. "I don't wanna de-escalate," she said, taking care to pronounce the word correctly.

And Alexa knew immediately what was going to happen next. She didn't even blink when Kelsey began to scream at the top of her lungs, "I want Alexa to stay! You're mean, Daddy! You're mean to send her away. She's going to make me better and you don't want me to get better! You hate me, and you hate Mommy and Alexa, too." Tears streamed down the child's cheeks. "I hate you, Daddy! I don't want to stay here anymore. I want to be with Mommy and Jack and Kyle. And if I can't go there, I'll go back to the hospital 'cause I won't stay here with you!"

Alexa saw the color drain from Ryan's face, saw the incredible hurt replace the anger in his eyes. She actually felt sorry for him. He looked sick, as if he'd been kicked in the head. Melissa rushed to her daughter's side and held her, rocking her in her arms, murmuring soothing words to her.

That child was a real piece of work, Alexa mused, both appalled and astonished by the success of Kelsey's manipulative abilities. She was under no delusions as to the girl's sudden affection for her. As a good tactician whose goal was to escalate hostility between her parents, keeping Alexa—the obstacle between them—was the practical stratagem.

Ryan caved in. "Kelsey, I understand that you're upset," he said softly, his voice raw with pain. "You must calm down, sweetheart. It's not good for you to get so worked up."

His daughter was clearly his Achilles' heel, the one person he couldn't seem to treat with cool detachment or distancing anger. Alexa knew those tactics of his well; she'd personally experienced both during her long-ago days as his lover. He allowed her to get only so close and then—wham!—it was as if a trapdoor slammed down between them, separating them while he withdrew from her. Their closest, most precious moments had been inevitably followed by a quarrel, initiated by Ryan.

"Kelsey, please stop crying and listen to me," Ryan coaxed.

Kelsey stopped crying. Instantly. The tears were gone, the wailing, the sobs. There was not even a lingering sniffle. She looked up at her father with those big, coffee-brown eyes of hers, that were so like his own.

"Kelsey, you know how much I love you and how much I want you to get well," Ryan continued quietly. "If you want Alexa as your physical therapist, of course you will have her."

"Thank you, Daddy," Kelsey said, smiling happily.

It was business as usual for her, Alexa guessed. Pit Mom against Dad, stage a scene and get whatever you want. At that moment, Kelsey seemed so formidable, it was hard to remember that she was a seriously injured child with desperate physical and emotional needs.

Alexa forced herself to remember. It was imperative to establish who was in charge here if a course of treatment was to be implemented—and succeed.

"There's just one thing we have to get straight before I agree to work with you, Kelsey," Alexa spoke up, her voice firm. "And that is, I can't be fired. I want a contract drawn up preventing anyone from terminating my services until I agree it's necessary."

"That's a really smart move," Melissa said admiringly. "Since Ryan hates you, he'd fire you at least once a day if you didn't have some sort of legal protection. He can be relentless."

It seemed to Alexa that the entire trio before her qualified as relentless. She looked directly at Kelsey. "The contract protects all of us. I don't want Kelsey to throw a scene and kick me out whenever she doesn't feel like doing the exercises that we're going to be doing."

"I'd never do that," Kelsey said earnestly, smiling angelically from her mother to her father.

"I'll have my attorney draw up the contract to be signed tomorrow," Ryan said, his voice as stiff and tense as his expression.

"I'd still like to get started today," Alexa said, feeling far less resolute than she sounded. But perseverance was essential in rehabilitation, and she was going to need a double dose of it to prevail in this case. "We don't have to use the equipment today. I'll go through some passive range-of-motion exercises with her."

"Kelsey and I will be waiting for you upstairs," Melissa said, whisking Kelsey and the wheelchair in the direction of the elevator. Alexa started to follow them.

"Just a minute, Alexa." Ryan's voice stopped her in her tracks.

She turned to face him. There was a brief awkward silence. Ryan cleared his throat. "Melissa said that I hated you. Like much of what she says, it's not true."

Alexa shrugged. "It's irrelevant."

"But what isn't irrelevant is *your* hatred of *me.* Despite this ironclad contract you insist upon, I won't tolerate you turning my child against me, Alexa."

She gaped at him, too shocked to be offended. While her mind scrambled for a response, Ryan continued his verbal onslaught. "Your showing up here today isn't merely a coincidence, is it? You asked Dr. Ellender to recommend you for the position and she did, knowing nothing of your ulterior motive. And you haven't wasted a moment since your arrival, have you, Alexa? You immediately befriended

Melissa and drew up the battle lines with my little girl squarely in the middle.''

Alexa gasped. ''Why on earth would I do that?''

''Revenge.'' Ryan's voice was cold and hard. ''You came here to get revenge.''

Three

"**R**evenge?" Alexa repeated, dumbfounded.

"You weren't happy when our relationship—" he paused and inhaled deeply "—ended two years ago."

"And you think I've been carrying a grudge against you all this time?" She was no longer stunned, she was enraged. "That I've been waiting for the opportunity to extract revenge on you for—for dumping me?"

"That isn't what happened," Ryan countered swiftly. "Not exactly."

"It's *exactly* what happened, so spare us both the euphemisms. In fact I'm surprised you, of all people, use them. In your comic strip you unmercifully ridicule any public figure who dares to utter them."

There could be no sugarcoating that dark day he'd told her he was through with her. Alexa remembered it too well, along with the ones that followed, first her stunned bewilderment and then the aching heartbreak. No, their relationship hadn't "ended." That implied a mutual agreement, a pallid winding down. Which wasn't what had happened at all. Out of the blue, without a hint of warning, Ryan Cassidy had told her he didn't want her anymore. He had used her and then discarded her like a tabloid he'd already read.

"You're obviously harboring a great deal of hostility," Ryan said with maddening insouciance. "I think my observation is right on the mark."

"You couldn't be more wrong! And no matter how I felt, I'd never use a child as a weapon!" Fury surged through her; she felt almost incoherent with rage. "Those are *your* tactics and Melissa's, not mine."

She began to pace back and forth, too agitated to stay still. "You have gravely insulted me. I've never let my personal feelings get in the way of my dealings with patients, and I'm not about to disregard my own professional and personal ethics because of *you!*"

She was shaking, she was so angry. Her face was flooded with hot color, her fists clenched. If she were a man—her brother Ben, for example—she knew she would've hauled off and socked Ryan Cassidy with every ounce of strength she possessed.

Certainly she had been insulted before, by both patients and their parents. It wasn't pleasant but she accepted it as part of the job, for there was a lot of displaced anger among people suffering both physical and emotional stress and strain. But this...what Ryan had said to her... She tried to remember if she'd ever been angrier, and couldn't. He'd struck some deeply hidden vulnerability within her to evoke such a wild response.

"If I've mistaken your motives, I apologize." Ryan cut into her reverie. But he didn't sound very sorry. His tone was almost flippant, his dark eyes challenging.

Alexa fought the urge to charge him like a defensive tackle and knock him to the ground. As kids, Ben had instructed both her and Carrie in such skills, then complained when they ganged up on him to win.

"There's another thing." She lighted into him verbally, since she had to forego the pleasure physically. "You're deluded if you believe for one second that I've been holding a grudge against you for two years. The idea of me wanting revenge on you is strictly a product of your monstrous ego and ridiculous imagination. I—I haven't given you a thought since the last time I saw you."

Ryan's eyes locked with hers. "I don't believe you."

"What?" A hot flush slowly suffused her cheeks.

"I said I don't believe you. I think you have thought about me these past two years."

"I heard what you said," Alexa snapped, regaining her composure somewhat. *Somewhat.* She was still blushing and her insides were churning. "I just couldn't believe you said it, that you're so incredibly vain that you think I've been carrying some kind of stupid torch for you all this time."

"I didn't say you were. But I do think you've thought of me."

Oh, she had. Far too often. But she decided that she would rather be struck by one of those lightning bolts flashing in the sky than to ever admit it. She opened her mouth to vigorously deny having had even a single thought about him ever, when Ryan stretched out his arm to touch her lips with his fingertips.

"Before you say anything, before you tear into me, let me tell you why I think what I do."

"I don't want to hear anything you have to say," Alexa cried, but her voice was not as strong, not as forceful as she wished. A sudden, shocking weakness had overtaken her. The movement of her lips against his fingers was so very intimate, the effect, erotic.

Ryan ignored her protest. "I know because I've thought of you, Alexa," he said quietly. Too many times, he added silently. Many more times than he'd wanted to.

He gazed down at her, drinking in the lovely pale blueness of her eyes, the well-shaped curve of her mouth. He remembered kissing her, watching the thick dark veil of her lashes close over her eyes as his mouth touched hers. He remembered the soft, alluring taste of her lips. Quite abruptly, his throat grew dry, his breathing became ragged.

Alexa skittered away from him, embarrassed by her jumpiness but unable to control it. Her lips were tingling from his touch. Even more disconcerting were the tiny hot sparks that seemed to ignite within her all at once, like spontaneous combustion. They blazed into an ache, a sharp physical longing so acute that it was almost painful. She felt the throbbing in her nipples, her stomach, deep between her legs.

Her response to Ryan's touch had always been immediate and explosive. And though she'd once gloried in her own sensuality so effortlessly aroused by him, she was now horrified by it. And by his continuing power over her.

"Stay away from me," she said huskily. "Don't touch me. I mean it, Ryan. Or I'll slap you with a—a sexual harassment suit so fast you won't know what hit you. And that's one area that's off-limits for jokes these days, even for an iconoclast like you."

"You think so?" Quick as lightning, he advanced toward her, grasping her elbows and pulling her around to face him. "But then again, your sense of humor is even weirder than mine. You make jokes about wheelchairs acting as lightning rods. About handicapped children getting electrocuted. If you ask me, *that's* the one taboo subject for comic strips, even for an iconoclastic one like mine."

"You've blown the whole thing out of proportion. I'd never make fun of the differently abled." She tried to jerk away from him, but his grip tightened and he slowly drew her toward him.

"What was that lecture you gave me about using euphemisms?" His other arm went around her waist, bringing her up against him. "Seems like I'm not the only guilty party."

"Let me go, Ryan." Alexa tried to use her hands as leverage to shove him away. It didn't work. His arms closed around her, strong as steel bands, his eyes holding hers, his gaze as powerful as his grip.

"I didn't come here for this," she whispered as his mouth descended slowly, inexorably to hers.

"Maybe not," Ryan said raspily. "But you want it as much as I do."

His mouth closed over hers and the hot, heady taste of him filled her as his tongue penetrated masterfully, deliciously. Alexa's senses spun. Instantaneously she was plunged back into the maelstrom of hot passion that had always burned between them. It had not cooled during the two-year hiatus. Sensual memories of their lovemaking swept over her, blending the past with the present, temporarily obliterating her defenses.

She moaned as their tongues rubbed seductively, and her arms crept slowly around his neck to hold him tight. Ryan arched her closer to him and she quivered at the thick, hard feel of him between her legs where she was already swollen and throbbing. He was fully, boldly aroused, moving against her with insistent male pressure. A syrupy warmth flowed through her, and she clung to him as her anchor in the swirling seas of sensuality.

Ryan felt the passionate wildness coursing through him. The taste and the touch and the feel of her went straight to his head like a mind-bending drug, taking over his thoughts and his actions, making him crave more and more.

She was warm and soft and sexy in his arms, and he kissed her with a deep, demanding hunger that grew and intensified until it had spiraled out of his control. The incendiary passion that had exploded between them the first time—and every time—he'd taken her in his arms was consuming him again.

It had been this way between them since he had first kissed her what seemed to be a lifetime ago. She'd made him want her, *need* her, the way he'd never wanted or needed a woman before. The profound urgency she evoked within him took him out of himself, shredding the deep reserve with which he shielded himself, torpedoing his normally steadfast control. An exhilarating but most disturbing phenomenon, one that he'd found irresistible yet threatening. A risk that, ultimately, he knew he dared not permanently take.

There was enough craziness in his life without adding the wild emotional highs loving Alexa induced; there were enough characters irrevocably stuck in his life who were capable of disrupting the ordered, controlled existence he craved without adding Alexa to the cast.

She was the one who, on a whim, could effortlessly turn his world upside down. True, she hadn't done so during the eight months they'd been together, but Ryan had recognized the full disaster potential. He'd cut her loose, he'd *had* to. His sense of self-preservation demanded it. And the ensuing sorrow and misery he'd experienced without her had only reinforced his sense of having done the right thing. Better to suffer now, than later. Or something like that...

Alexa felt the heat of his big hands moving over her, strong and demanding, and when he cupped her breast, she leaned into his hand, encouraging the caress of his long lean fingers. He began a slow sensual massage, rubbing her nipple, which had already peaked and was straining against the soft cotton fabric of her shirt.

A streak of fire radiated from his fingertips to the hot moist core of her. The sensation was electrifying. She knew this burning, intense need but it had been a long time since she had experienced it. Two long, lonely years since she had experienced it. Two long, lonely years since she'd been in his arms, wanting him, loving him...

Wanting him... *Loving him?* It was the mindless drifting of her own thoughts that shocked her out of the sensual, voluptuous daze engulfing her. *She did not love this man! She couldn't—she wouldn't!* Bad enough she had fallen victim to the power of his charm and rampant sexuality once, but to do so twice was unthinkable, unforgivable. At least she'd had the excuse of ignorance the first time around. No longer. Now she knew his character—or the lack of it. She was not some masochistic little twit to be used and then betrayed over and over again.

Both angered and alarmed by the desire he had so easily aroused in her, and aghast at the treachery of her own mind—*loving him, indeed!*—Alexa jerked her mouth from his and pushed against his shoulders. She could feel the hard, heavy muscles beneath her palms. Once again, a feminine thrill rocked her. This time Alexa steeled herself against it, against the potent appeal of his uncompromising masculinity.

"Just what are you trying to prove, Ryan?" she lashed out, launching her preemptive strike before he could seize the offensive. "That any female who comes within your range is fair game? Do you have a compulsive need to make a pass at every woman you see?"

"The answer to your last two questions is a resounding 'no.'" Ryan intended to sound casual and mocking. But the raw edge of his voice betrayed his inner turmoil.

"I wasn't trying to prove anything," he added, striving for equanimity. He was badly shaken by how swiftly and thoroughly his control had been undone by their kiss. He never should have touched her; the very fact that he'd been unable to stop himself didn't augur well for his self-control in her presence. If anything, he was even more susceptible to her now than he'd been two years ago.

"I'm going to tell you this just one more time. Keep away from me!" Alexa said sharply. She was horrified that the huskiness in his voice sent responsive shivers tingling through her body. She knew she was in trouble when merely his voice could affect her so. And when she looked into the stormy darkness of his eyes . . .

Alexa quickly averted her gaze. It was not going to happen again, she promised herself. She was not going to fall under his sexual spell, not this time. The first time had been understandable enough. When she had first met Ryan Cassidy, she'd been the stereotypical trusting, naive virgin—a bit overaged, perhaps—but waiting for the love of her life to come along, believing that once she'd found him, their love would last forever.

She'd had no defenses back then; she'd been a woefully easy score for a smooth-talking, master manipulator like Ryan. After her affair with him, she had evolved into yet another stereotype, the classic sadder-but-wiser woman.

Now she was wary and guarded and not at all certain that she even believed in lasting love. Oh, there were a few existing cases, she had to concede, her parents' long marriage being one. She hoped her sister Carrie's year-old marriage to Tyler Tremaine would turn out to be another.

But she had no such hope or expectations for herself. There was nothing special or unique or inherently lovable about her that would inspire a man to want to mate with her for life. The man standing before her had taught her that.

"I'm going upstairs to work with Kelsey now," she announced, walking away from him. "Whether you believe it or not, she is the only reason I'm here."

"I want to believe it," Ryan said quietly.

Alexa stopped in her tracks, then whirled around to glare at him. "Oh, spare me that heartrending, wistful note in your voice. I admit it's quite effective. You're a talented actor and I bought your performance once before, but I'm not stupid enough to fall for the same schtick again."

"What do you mean by that ?" There was not a trace of anything heartrending or wistful in Ryan's tone now.

Alexa raised her chin and faced him defiantly. "I mean I've heard it before, your lonely, tortured, afraid-to-trust-a-woman-because-you-lost-your-mother-at-an-early-age-and-now-fear-abandonment routine."

Ryan felt a peculiar tightening in his chest. He'd confided things to her that he had never told another living soul, and she thought it had all been a calculating "routine"? Well, maybe it was better that she did. He had regretted those intimate confessions to her, but never more so than now.

"There are a lot of people who have survived the childhood loss of a parent and don't use their loss to manipulate others or to justify their own rotten behavior, Ryan," Alexa continued, unaware of his inner turmoil. "My sister Carrie's husband is one. His mother was killed in a car accident when he was only five but—"

"Yes, I'd heard that Carrie married Tyler Tremaine," Ryan cut in. He was eager to shift the focus from himself to someone—anyone!—else. "That news spread through the city like a forest fire in a windy canyon. It isn't often that a young widow with toddler triplets manages to snag herself one of the most eligible bachelors around."

"Carrie did not *snag* Tyler," Alexa snapped. "Although it's entirely in character for a coldhearted cynic like you to see it that way. They love each other very much, and Tyler loves Carrie's children, too. He's already petitioned to adopt them."

She braced herself for some cynically caustic remark about the spectacular advantages of becoming a Tremaine heir, whether by birth or by *snagging* the position through adoption.

To her surprise, Ryan merely shrugged and said quite civilly, "Well, I'm happy for Carrie. I always liked her, and I thought it was tragic for her to be widowed at such a young age with infant triplets. I'm glad things worked out for them all. For Tyler, too. I don't know him well, but he seems like a good guy."

"He's a wonderful man," Alexa said loyally.

"I imagine your brother Ben must be thrilled with that match," Ryan said dryly.

Alexa flushed. "The whole family is happy about it. Why wouldn't we be?"

"But Ben must be positively euphoric, given his reverence for money and status."

Alexa scowled. Unfortunately there was no refuting that statement. Still, the amusement in his tone rankled. "If you think I'm going to stand around and let you insult my brother, you're mistaken,'' she said coldly, seizing the offensive once again.

''I didn't mean to insult him, I was just stating a fact. I know Ben, remember?''

''Yes, you knew my brother and my sister and her babies and our parents and most of my friends. I introduced them to you and we spent time with them all.''

''When you know one of the Shaw triplets, you end up knowing everyone else who knows them too,'' Ryan said lightly. ''A most gregarious trio.''

''No one could ever accuse you of being gregarious.'' Alexa stared at him with ice blue eyes. ''Or honest. You knew everyone in my life but you never even bothered to mention the existence of your own child. Which is why I couldn't have lobbied Dr. Ellender for this case. I didn't even know you had a daughter.''

The attack was so unexpected that Ryan was caught completely off guard. He had no glib comeback. ''I—I didn't think we would last as long as we did, so at first it seemed easier not to bring Kelsey into it. Once we became more deeply involved, I realized that you should know about her but...''

''You chose not to tell me.''

''I wasn't sure how,'' he blurted. ''It's a bit awkward to announce six months into a relationship, 'Oh, by the way, honey, I have a little girl'. I mean, it's hardly a fact that would've slipped my mind, now is it? I thought it through. You would've probed for some dark hidden motive and accused me of deception. So rather than making excuses, I just kept the part of my life with Kelsey separate from my time with you.''

''You always did have a talent for compartmentalizing,'' Alexa said acidly.

''I admit to leading a very compartmentalized life.'' Ryan lapsed into the flippancy that she hated. ''That was one of your chief complaints about me back then.''

"Well, my chief complaint about you now is that you're on the same planet that I'm on."

His lips twitched. "I'm afraid there's nothing much I can do about that, but I will try to stay out of your way while you're here."

"You do that." Alexa marched up the grand staircase. It made for a ridiculously dramatic exit. She was certain that Ryan was standing below snickering, but she held her head high and didn't look back.

"Good morning, Kelsey!" Alexa said cheerfully as she strode briskly into the child's bedroom. "I hope you'll note that I arrived well before your program airs. Are you ready to work?"

Kelsey, in a kelly green sweat suit with a pair of pandas romping across the front of the shirt, was dressing a Barbie doll. A pile of dolls and doll clothes were strewed all over the bed. Beside the bed, a portly graying woman was brushing the little girl's hair. The older woman jumped, gasped, and muttered something in another language. Spanish, Alexa guessed.

"I'm sorry to startle you," Alexa said. "The maid let me in and I told her I knew my way to Kelsey's room. I'm Alexa Shaw, the physical therapist who'll be working with Kelsey."

"Gloria Martinez. I spoke to you on the telephone the other day. I'm taking care of Kelsey until she's back on her feet—and back in school." The nurse smiled encouragingly at Kelsey.

Kelsey scowled. "I'm not going back to school until I'm exactly like I was before."

Alexa stood beside the bed and reached for Kelsey's foot. It lay cool and still in her hands and she began to rotate the rigid ball joint. "How often does the school's homebound tutor come to the house for lessons?"

"*Too* often," grumbled Kelsey. "I hate tutors."

Gloria rolled her eyes and murmured another few Spanish phrases. "She's had four tutors since the beginning of September. Two refused to come back, and two were told never to come back." The nurse shook her head. "The school district is running out of people to send over."

Kelsey smiled for the first time since Alexa's arrival. "We scared the first two away, Daddy hated the third one and Mommy hated the fourth. The fifth one is coming next week. I bet we'll get rid of her, too."

"I can see that schoolwork is not a high priority around here," Alexa observed, taking the child's other foot to repeat the ministrations.

"It's difficult for Kelsey to maintain an interest in her schoolwork with so much else on her mind." Ryan's voice sounded from the threshold, startling them all.

Alexa nearly dropped Kelsey's foot. Fortunately she managed to hang on to it and resume the exercises without pause. Gloria gave a small shriek. "Everybody is sneaking around today," the nurse accused crossly. "It is not good for my nerves."

"Hi, Daddy!" Kelsey smiled adorably at Ryan. "I thought you said you were working all morning and I wouldn't see you till lunchtime."

"I am." Ryan cleared his throat and stole a quick glance at Alexa, lithe and trim in jeans and a royal blue cotton shirt. The darker blue of her shirt accentuated the paleness of her eyes, a fascinating contrast. His looked at her again, his gaze lingering. She was a pleasure to behold, so strong and sure, so beautiful.

Alexa seemed unaware of him. She was concentrating on her passive exercise regimen with Kelsey's limbs. Ryan felt both Kelsey's and Gloria's curious stares, and felt the need to justify his presence. "That is, I *was* working until I heard the doorbell and the maid told me that—uh—your physical therapist had arrived. I have that contract and it needs to be signed."

"Alexa said she had to have a special contract so she couldn't get fired," Kelsey explained chattily to Gloria.

Ryan handed the contract and a pen to Alexa who hastily scrawled her name.

"Witness this, will you, Gloria?" asked Ryan, this time giving the paper and pen to the nurse.

"I want to sign, too," insisted Kelsey. Ryan indulged her, allowing her to write Kelsey Lynn Cassidy under Alexa's name on the document.

Gloria signed her name, then stared archly from Ryan to Kelsey. "Too bad one of those tutors didn't insist on something like this. Then this child would be learning something instead of watching TV and playing all day long."

The acerbic condemnation in the older woman's tone was unmistakable and took Alexa by surprise. She felt respect for her plain-speaking, along with a certain sense of dread. The Cassidys were hardly a convivial group, welcoming a dissenting opinion. Would the nurse go the way of the hapless tutors?

Apparently not. Ryan merely chuckled. "Kelsey isn't wasting her time. She plays lots of video games and they're supposed to promote good hand-eye coordination, aren't they? And you can never underestimate the value of her creative play with her dolls and stuff."

He was talking to Gloria, but watching Alexa's reaction. As far as he could tell, she had none; her face remained neutrally blank. He had no idea of the effort she was expending in keeping it so. "Am I right, Alexa?" he asked, wanting, needing some response.

"No schoolwork versus playing all day?" Alexa said thoughtfully. She tried and failed to keep the ironic edge from her tone. "Oh, I think we all know the answer to that one."

Put like that, his theory sounded ridiculous. Which he knew it was. Ryan heaved a sigh. "Well, we'll find someone who has both the sensitivity and the ability to teach Kelsey. It's . . . just taking a little time, that's all."

"You'll never find anyone who will get the stamp of approval from both you and Melissa," Gloria said darkly. "It doesn't matter who walks in the door—one of you will side for, the other against. The two of you would take sides against the saints themselves."

"That's what happened with Alexa," Kelsey said brightly. "Mommy liked her and Daddy hated her. But here she is."

"Kelsey, I do not hate her," Ryan muttered through clenched teeth.

"I bet she hates you, though," Kelsey sang out. "Right, Alexa?"

"Don't answer," Gloria advised. "Don't let any of them drag you into any of their arguments, because it's like being stuck in quicksand. You'll be weighted down and sink from sight and they'll simply continue fighting. I know. I've been dealing with the Cassidys for the past forty years. Ryan's mother—dear Isabella, God rest her soul—was my cousin. We were close as twins, went through nursing school together, were in each other's weddings. She died when Ryan was just ten years old. Ah, what a tragedy!"

"Gloria, tell me how Daddy ran away and hid and no one could find him after Grandma Isabella's funeral," Kelsey demanded eagerly, her brown eyes rapt. "You know, how he was hiding in that creepy mausoleum on the other side of the cemetery till nighttime and it got dark and he was still missing and everybody went looking for—"

"Kelsey, that's enough!" Ryan interrupted, appalled.

It didn't surprise Alexa that Kelsey seemed to relish the tale. A dark and ghoulish reminiscence seemed more her style than the Babysitters Club books so many young girls her age favored.

"Gloria, you never should have told her that!" Ryan thundered. His face was a deep dark red. "I've never told anyone. It's a—a very private memory."

Alexa glanced at him curiously. He had told her that story himself two years ago, and she had listened with tears in her eyes as she'd pictured the grief-stricken, motherless child hiding alone and desolate in the mausoleum, as if his presence there could somehow will his mother to return.

After their breakup, distrusting and disillusioned, she had guessed that he told that tear-jerking tale to each and every one of his new conquests. After all, it had a powerful effect. What warmhearted woman, already in love with him, could resist putting her arms around him in a comforting embrace? She flushed, remembering. Her need to comfort him had led them straight to his bedroom. Quickly she blocked the memory and zeroed back into the scene at hand.

Ryan was lecturing Gloria who merely shrugged, totally unintimidated by his wrath. "Kelsey loves hearing old family stories, especially ones of you as a boy. And I want her to know about her grandmother, my dearest Isabella. *You* never mention her to the child, and people only live on through the memories handed down from generation to generation."

"You can tell her about her grandmother, but kindly leave me out of your tales," Ryan said stiffly.

Gloria muttered a few Spanish words, and though Alexa did not know their meaning, the nurse's body language was clear enough. She was quite certain that Kelsey Cassidy would continue to hear whatever family stories Gloria Martinez wanted to tell her.

"Did you see any ghosts or vampires in the cemetery that night, Daddy?" Kelsey asked cheerfully. "Since they only come out at night and you were right there in a real *crypt*—"

"The subject is closed, Kelsey," Ryan said in a startlingly firm voice, quite unlike the placating, fulsome tones Alexa had previously heard him use with the child.

"But I wanna—" Kelsey began.

Alexa decided to try to ward off another skirmish. "We have work to do," she said briskly. "No ghosts or vampires allowed. Now let's see you reach for that trapeze and see how strong you are, Kelsey."

Kelsey stretched her arms up and grabbed the trapeze. Ryan's breath caught in his throat. "Kelsey, honey, be caref—"

"Out with you!" Gloria ordered, taking his arm and giving him a forceful tug. "They don't need us in here. Let this girl do the work she came here to do."

Alexa kept her attention focused on Kelsey who was gripping the trapeze and pulling herself higher in the bed. "You're the one doing the work, Kelsey," she said encouragingly. "And you're off to a terrific start."

Kelsey smiled slightly, but she was concentrating fiercely on her task.

Though Gloria left the room, Ryan remained beside the bed, watching his daughter. He seemed to be holding his breath as she went through the motions directed by Alexa.

He didn't say a word until Alexa, sensing Kelsey's waning interest and flagging energy, suggested a break some twenty minutes later. "While Gloria gets Kelsey a drink, I'd like to show you the equipment I've rented for Kelsey," Ryan said to Alexa.

Alexa reluctantly followed him out of the room and down the hall. Involuntarily her eyes flicked over the back of him, along the tall strong lines of his body. He was wearing jeans that molded his taut buttocks and long lean thighs in a most sex-defining way. They fit his front equally well, Alexa knew. She'd spent the past twenty minutes, dragging her wayward eyes away from him. His blue chambray shirt looked soft and comfortable, casually emphasizing his broad shoulders and chest.

Alexa gulped. No, she did not want to be alone with him, not when her every nerve was tingling with awareness of him. Squaring her shoulders, she reminded herself that she was a professional who could not permit her own personal feelings to interfere with her patient's welfare.

"Kelsey has a lot of determination," she said, striving for normalcy. Breaking this charged silence between them was a step in that direction. "If she uses it to work toward re-habilitation, she will make remarkable progress."

"That sounds like standard PT patter," Ryan said trenchantly. "Substitute the name and you have the all-purpose pep talk delivered to the concerned relatives of all your patients."

Alexa clenched her jaw. "Fine. From now on, I'll keep my patient progress observations to myself and have the doctor submit the written records to you."

"I don't want that," Ryan gritted. "But I don't like to hear you talk about Kelsey as if she's just any patient. Kelsey is special."

"*All* my patients are special," Alexa said resolutely.

Ryan heaved a sigh. "Look, I don't want to argue with you . . ." His voice trailed off. Actually, that's exactly what he wanted to do—to argue with her and keep that wall of hostility firmly entrenched between them.

That kiss they had shared yesterday, so brief yet so hot and intimate, had had an effect upon him that lingered still. He'd spent a good deal of last night tossing and turning in his bed, until he'd given up the idea of sleep and given in to the restless urge to pace aimlessly through the dark, quiet house.

All through that long tumultuous night, he kept trying to delude himself into believing it was strictly sexual hunger, the impersonal yet demanding male need for a woman. *Any* woman. After all, his sex life had been nonexistent since Kelsey's accident, and irregular and unenthusiastic before that.

But, ultimately, he couldn't fool himself into believing it. It was Alexa, only Alexa, who had this effect on him. Alexa made him need and want and feel when he tried not to; she evoked emotions he was determined to deny. As desperately as he wanted to send her away, he wanted to reach for her and keep her close.

He'd sent her away once before. And now she was back, haunting his nights and his days. He hadn't been able to do a thing in his studio this morning, knowing that she would be here today. He hadn't drawn a line or written a word; his usually unfailing sense of the ridiculous that guided every comic frame was absent. His every mental sensor had been primed and waiting for her appearance.

A sense of desperation, anger mixed with impatience, surged through him. And this was only her first day on the job. *Things just couldn't go on this way!*

He opened the door to a room at the end of the corridor and motioned her inside. Alexa gazed at her surroundings with wide blue eyes. The entire outer wall was comprised of floor-to-ceiling windows with a glass door in the middle of the panes. There was a balcony outside overlooking a kidney-shaped swimming pool, surrounded by a *faux* grotto setting.

"This was to be an exercise room, a private gym, if you will," Ryan said, indicating the StairMaster and the Life-cycle and a couple other pieces she couldn't immediately identify. "There is a spiral staircase off the balcony leading down to the pool." His voice challenged her to comment.

At any other time, Alexa would have; that grotto was truly hilarious, a touch of the South Pacific completed the around-the-world decorating theme. But she had seen the rehabilitative equipment scattered among the standard exercise things. There was a mat and mat table and a set of parallel bars and virtually every other piece of therapeutic equipment Kelsey would need during her course of therapy.

"This room is as well equipped as the one in our professional building. It could hold its own with the hospital's PT department," she said, awed.

"I rented it all from a medical supply company so Kelsey wouldn't have to go to that Children's Rehabilitation Institute that the doctors seemed so sold on."

"It's a terrific place," Alexa said quickly. "I work there as a volunteer twice a week."

"After spending two and a half months in a hospital, I didn't want my child to go to any institute. That's mere shorthand for *institution*," he added grimly.

"You make it sound like some hellhole out of Dickens. It's not, I assure you," Alexa exclaimed. "And though I can understand you wanting to have Kelsey at home, there are definite advantages to living at the rehab center during the recovery period. At CRI, she would be with other children, following a structured course of study and therapy and play. Here she is isolated and outrageously spoiled and—"

"You're calling my child spoiled?" Ryan cut in indignantly.

"And then some," Alexa replied, not backing down. She was used to laying out cold hard facts and then dealing with them. In her line of work, there could be no comfortable self-delusion or denial. "Furthermore, you know it, though you certainly don't like hearing it, do you?"

"You *are* in cahoots with Melissa! I knew it! You both want to put Kelsey in that place and are willing to say anything—even slander the poor little girl—to bolster your case."

"If Melissa wanted Kelsey to go to Children's Rehab, I can understand why, but I'm certainly not in *cahoots* with her," Alexa said scornfully. "I only met her for the first time yesterday."

She gave her head a shake and grimaced. "You're defensive and paranoid, Ryan. A miserable combination. And why, I wonder? Because deep down you know that keeping Kelsey here and allowing her to get away with murder isn't really what's best for her? Because you feel guilty for the custody fight you're planning? Or guilty because you couldn't prevent the accident in the first place and your child was hurt?"

Fury erupted within him with volcanic force. "I refuse to listen to such...such insulting psycho-babble tripe! I won't have it, not here in my own house! I don't have to put up with it or with you! As of this moment, you're fired!''

Alexa folded her arms and gazed at him, her blue eyes steely. ''You can't fire me. I have a contract that says so.''

Four

Ryan tried to rein in his temper. Sometimes a touch of condescending amusement could be far more effective than outrage. "Contracts can be broken, particularly one that was drawn up by my own lawyer. You didn't bother to read what you signed, Alexa."

It was a bluff but a good one, he thought. "That not only shows poor business skills, but also a lamentable lack of common sense." His supercilious tone was guaranteed to infuriate.

Alexa was infuriated, all right. But dealing with her brother Ben's rather devious machinations through the years stood her in good stead. She'd learned a few things about devious dealings herself.

"I didn't have to read it," she replied, trying to match his tone note for obnoxious note. "Because no matter what sneaky loophole you and your lawyer might've stuck in there, the contract I signed will be upheld, I'll make sure of that. So don't even think about trying to break it."

"Why not? Will you sue me?" He laughed scornfully.

"You don't think I would?"

"No." He stared down at her. She was maddening, headstrong and confident. He was furious with her. But she was so damn beautiful, so desirable. A shudder of pure male need passed through him but he rebelled against it, didn't let himself give in to it. He wanted her so much; he had to get rid of her!

"You wouldn't sue me," he repeated, his lips drawn into a menacing smile.

"Oh yes I would," Alexa assured him. "I take my professional responsibilities very seriously. I wanted that contract to protect my therapeutic relationship with Kelsey, and I'll do whatever it takes to enforce it."

"That means hiring a lawyer, going to court, investing a lot of time and money in a suit you'll undoubtedly lose."

But even as he made the threat, Ryan knew he was not going to force the issue. Part of him admired her tenacity on behalf of her patient. After all, when it came to dealing with Kelsey, a cringing shrinking violet who folded at challenge would get nowhere. Still, he was not going to easily concede. Let her sweat it out a little!

But Alexa was not about to be bullied. "The situation you're describing is your own," she said coolly. "I have no intention of losing anything. One word to my sister Carrie and I'll have the power of Tremaine Incorporated behind me. They can afford the best legal talent in any area of the law. I'll win, Ryan. Don't ever doubt it."

Inwardly she was cringing. She sounded like Ben off on one of his The-Tremaines-And-Me tangents! But the circumstances warranted it, and Ryan didn't need to know that she had no intention of involving the Tremaines in this fight.

"You're threatening me with the Tremaines?" Ryan was stunned. And outraged. This was their own private war; dragging in allies was a twist he hadn't anticipated.

"I don't like threats, so let's just consider it a promise instead," Alexa replied. She even managed to look and sound condescendingly amused.

Ryan could almost hear the gong sound. She'd definitely won this round.

"Promise, threat, whatever. The Tremaines are a potent weapon," called an excited, delighted voice from the other side of the room.

Both Alexa and Ryan whirled around to see Melissa enter the room, pushing a wide-eyed Kelsey in her wheelchair.

Ryan stifled the snarl welling in his throat. His patience and control were hanging by a thread. First, the specter of the Tremaines and now Melissa, too! All that was needed to complete the scene was his dear old dad accompanied by Wives Two, Three and Four and the assorted step-siblings. It was moments like this when he was sure he was living in one of his own bizarre comic-strip storylines.

"So it's finally happened!" Melissa exclaimed gleefully. "Ryan Cassidy finally met somebody he can't charm or walk all over! *She* has the Tremaines on her side, and they can buy and sell you a hundred times over, Ryan. They can hire one hundred lawyers to your every one, they can—"

"Uh, we get the picture, Melissa," Alexa cut in, feeling heartily embarrassed by the proxy boasts.

"You can't fire Alexa, Daddy," Kelsey piped up. "Me and Gloria signed the contract, remember?"

"I remember, sweetheart," Ryan said tightly. "If you'll excuse me, I have work to do."

He strode from the room, heading toward his studio. It was not a retreat, though he was certain that his former wife and his former girlfriend probably thought so. It was ironic those two had paired up. They were so very different— Melissa manipulative and melodramatic, Alexa warm and competent, honest and open.

Ryan scowled at the direction his thoughts were taking. He would not think of Alexa. Anyway, she seemed to have taken some lessons from Melissa in the art of melodramatic manipulation. Threatening him with the power of the Tremaines!

"So how did you get the Tremaines on your side?" Melissa demanded of Alexa. "Or were you just bluffing?"

Still embarrassed by her braggadocio, Alexa mentioned Carrie's marriage to Tyler Tremaine. She didn't want anyone thinking Carrie had married Tyler for his money, so she added that Carrie had been previously widowed and that Tyler was a devoted stepfather to her two-and-a-half-year-old triplets, Dylan, Emily and Franklin. Soon he would be their legally adoptive father.

"Your sister has three two-year-olds!" Melissa marveled. "Kelsey, can you imagine if there were *three* of Kyle!"

Alexa assisted Kelsey onto the mat table for another exercise regimen. "My little brother Kyle is two. He's sort of a maniac sometimes, but I really miss him," Kelsey added softly.

"Kyle is crazy about Kelsey, and she's like a little mother to him," Melissa said. Her face hardened. "If she'd gone to the children's rehab place like I wanted her to, he could visit her. I would've brought him to see her every day."

"Why can't he visit her here?" Alexa asked. She realized she'd detonated an issue as volatile as a live grenade by the glances Melissa and Kelsey exchanged.

"Daddy says that Kyle can't come to his house," Kelsey said. "I couldn't get him to change his mind." She narrowed her eyes, scowling. "No matter what I did."

Alexa imagined the girl had certainly given it her best shot. Undoubtedly the tantrum she'd thrown had been one for the ages. But it hadn't worked?

"Ryan won't let Jack or Kyle on his property," Melissa's voice rose. "Knowing him, he'd have us arrested for trespassing if I dared to bring the baby here against his wishes. It all seems so hopeless." She rubbed her watering eyes, then fixed them intently on Alexa. The tears abruptly disappeared. "Until now, that is. With you on our side, we have a chance to win, Alexa."

Alexa was going through a routine to stretch Kelsey's calf muscles, first the left leg, then the right. "I'm afraid not even the Tremaines can force Ryan into inviting visitors he doesn't want into his own house."

"But *you* can help us, Alexa!" Melissa cried. "You're the only one who hasn't fallen under Ryan's spell. Finally there is someone who thinks that *I'm* worth helping."

"Melissa, of course you're worth helping. But I really don't know what I can do."

"Let's begin with the problem of Kyle not being allowed in here to visit Kelsey," suggested Melissa. "Does anyone have any ideas how to sneak him into the house?"

Both Melissa and Kelsey looked expectantly at Alexa. Alexa swallowed back a groan. Gloria Martinez had been right on the money with her quicksand analogy. She felt as if she were already stuck in a bog of it and each word she used to disentangle herself merely sucked her in deeper.

Alexa ended Kelsey's session shortly before noon. She had just enough time to grab a quick bite of lunch and then it was back to the professional building where she had a full afternoon scheduled with young patients in the gymnasium-size rooms whose facilities she shared with several other therapists.

Melissa insisted on walking her to her car. "Alexa, I want to thank you for finding a way to get Kelsey and Kyle together. I just know our plan is going to work," she said brightly, scurrying to keep up with Alexa's longer, faster strides.

Alexa thought of "their plan" and tried to calm the sudden churning of her stomach. Why had she allowed herself to get roped into this? Worse, she was the one who had actually come up with the scheme, not Melissa or Kelsey. It was growing up with a natural-born schemer like Ben, Alexa decided grimly. Some of it was bound to rub off.

"I strongly believe in siblings visiting each other during hospitalization. And of course, maintaining the sibling bond is just as vitally important during the convalescent period," Alexa said. She knew she sounded like a mental-health pamphlet. Did she also sound as if she were rehearsing what she was going to say to Ryan if they got caught? She gulped.

"I agree," Melissa said staunchly. "I brought Kyle to the hospital to see Kelsey as often as I could—whenever Ryan wasn't around, of course. The pediatric unit encouraged sisters and brothers to visit." She frowned. "Being an only child, Ryan doesn't know how it is between sisters and brothers. I mean, there wasn't much of a sibling bond between him and those trashy stepsisters of his and—"

"Ryan had stepsisters?" Alexa asked, curious in spite of herself. And they were trashy ones? "I knew he had a holy terror of a stepbrother, but never stepsisters."

Melissa stopped and stared at her strangely. "Ryan told you about his stepbrother?"

Alexa felt a surge of color suffuse her cheeks. She was certain that telling Melissa about her own past with Ryan would be a dreadful mistake. "Well no," she prevaricated, thinking fast. "I sort of overheard Gloria mention it."

"Ryan doesn't tell anybody about that stepbrother," Melissa confided. "I only heard about him from Gloria and his father. The boy was the son of Ryan's first stepmother and he made life hell for Ryan." She smiled nastily. "Too bad he's not around now to put Ryan through hell all over again."

"What about the stepsisters?" Alexa asked. Common sense told her she should not be talking about Ryan. She should not be interested in anything concerning him, not his past nor his present nor his future. Unfortunately her curiosity about him overruled her common sense and kept her listening avidly to Melissa.

"There were three of them, from his dad's third marriage," Melissa explained. "I met them a couple times when I was picking up and dropping off Kelsey. What trampy little airheads they were! And the most incredible thing is that

Ryan's father actually ran off with one of them! I mean, it's like Hollywood or something, isn't it? Eloping with your own stepdaughter!''

Alexa's jaw dropped. She hadn't heard that tale. She remembered feeling terribly sorry for the child Ryan had been when he'd told her about the cold cruel woman his father had married just a year after his mother's tragic death. Part of the package had been the woman's sociopathic son, a year older than Ryan who had a penchant for fighting, lying, stealing and setting fires. Eventually the couple divorced and Ryan, no longer a child, gained yet another stepmother. But he hadn't mentioned that his father had married a daughter of the third wife!

Melissa studied Alexa's shocked expression with approval. "You can see why I don't think Ryan has any right to condemn me for having a baby without being married to its father. Not with his own kinky family history! And I'd marry Jack in a second, if only I could.''

Alexa compared her own family situation—loving parents, close ties to her sister and brother who were her friends as well as her siblings—to Ryan's. She felt a surge of sympathy for him. The sadistic stepbrother story and the sordid stepsister tale were both unsavory episodes. Who could blame Ryan for only meting out selected chapters in his history?

The two women reached Alexa's car and paused alongside it.

"Jack Webber is the only man I've ever really loved,'' Melissa was saying plaintively. "But he went through a bitter divorce and he doesn't want to risk marriage again. I think he came close to marrying me last year but then he lost his job. It was a real blow to his pride, and the only work he's been able to find since is shift work in a fast-food restaurant. Then there was Kelsey's accident. Jack blames himself, and Ryan blames him, too.'' She burst into tears. "I don't know what I'm going to do, Alexa. Everything is falling apart. Now Ryan has decided to get custody of Kelsey and—''

"I don't think you have to worry about that." Alexa cut in, placing a comforting arm around Melissa's shoulders. "The courts usually favor the mother, don't they?"

"I've had custody of Kelsey ever since she was a baby." Melissa sobbed. "Ryan and I were divorced when she was four months old. He visited Kelsey every Wednesday evening and every Sunday afternoon until she was three years old, and then she started spending every other Saturday night with him at his place. To his credit, I suppose, he never missed a visit."

Melissa paused and frowned thoughtfully. "Except for a period of several months about two years ago. I think Ryan must've had some hot and heavy fling going back then because he did cancel quite a few of Kelsey's Saturday night visits. He'd only take her overnight about once a month and would see her just a few hours on Sunday afternoons."

Alexa went very still, remembering those mysterious Saturday nights and Sunday afternoons when Ryan would suddenly cancel plans they'd made—or refuse to make them in the first place. He wouldn't say why and she would suspect the worst, accusing him of seeing another woman, of being bored with her. She'd wanted to be with him all the time and to know exactly where he was and what he was doing every moment they were apart.

The memory of her own insecurity made Alexa wince. She'd been jealous and possessive and had become even more so as Ryan withdrew and became more evasive. If only he would have told her that he had a child! She would have understood. Had he thought she wouldn't? Had she appeared *that* possessive and insecure to him?

"Anyway, I guess Ryan's hot affair must've burned out after a time because he resumed his usual visiting schedule with Kelsey." Melissa scowled. "I'd like to believe that the woman involved dropped him flat and broke his heart, but I guess that's impossible because he doesn't have a heart."

"There is so much animosity between you and Ryan," Alexa said softly.

"How true. You'd think we'd had one of those fiery love-hate relationships, full of passion." Melissa shook her head. "Unfortunately it wasn't like that at all. We sort of stumbled into each other's lives at a bad period for both of us. We didn't have anything in common, we never even really liked each other very much. It was one of those things that should've been over and quickly forgotten—and it would have been—if we hadn't been careless one time."

"Kelsey?" Alexa murmured.

Melissa nodded. "Ryan insisted on marrying me, though neither of us even pretended we'd ever loved each other. When I got pregnant with Kyle, Ryan accused me of doing it deliberately, of using pregnancy to trap a man again. He talked about suing for custody of Kelsey then, but he didn't follow through. I know I'm not going to be so lucky this time!"

"You've logged a lot of hours taking care of that child alone through the years, Melissa," Alexa said soothingly. "I know I'm not a lawyer, but I just don't see why any judge would give custody of Kelsey to Ryan at this point."

"Ryan's lawyer could cite my unstable home situation," Melissa said bitterly. "I live with a man I'm not married to, and I have a child by him. I have to work—I'm a hostess at Hyland's Restaurant—because Jack and I need two incomes. As it is, we're barely scraping by and Ryan's loaded. Then there's Ryan's trump card. The one that's going to win him custody of my little girl. His stay-at-home wife."

"*His wife?*" Alexa gasped.

"Ryan is getting married." Melissa began to cry in earnest. "And his wife will be at home full-time to take care of Kelsey. It's a no-win situation for me. The Legal Aid lawyer I talked with knows of a number of cases where the ex-wife lost custody of her children because she had to work and the children's father had a new stay-at-home wife to look after them."

Ryan was getting married! Alexa's mind was reeling. The news was affecting her physically, making her feel both hot and cold, causing her breath to catch in her throat, choking her. She remembered how he had pulled her into his arms— just yesterday!—the way he had kissed her, and her own treacherous wanton response.

He had kissed her and he was getting married! Rage rushed through Alexa like the reviving force of a straight shot of adrenaline. *He was planning to marry another woman yet he had dared to kiss her!* Air filled her lungs with a whoosh and suddenly she was filled with what felt like superhuman strength. And resolve. Never had she thirsted so urgently for revenge.

"Melissa, you are not going to lose your daughter," Alexa promised so firmly and unequivocally that Melissa stopped crying and looked at her with a kind of dazed hope in her eyes. "I will do everything I can to help you keep Kelsey. Everything is going to be all right. You can count on that."

"Up! Up! Ride horsie!" demanded two-and-a-half-year-old Franklin as he tried to climb onto the big, bright carousel horse in Kelsey's bedroom.

Alexa picked up her nephew and put him on the horse, for at least the thirty-fifth time that morning. Unfortunately, once astride, Franklin found the horse too dull for his tastes. It didn't move or make a noise so he supplied his own motion and sound effects. Then he got bored. "Down! No ride horsie, Franklin down!"

"Hang on, I'll be over in a minute," Alexa called from across the room where she was trying to keep her niece, Emily, from demolishing the dollhouse. The delicate wooden furniture was not made for toddler play. Emily held up yet another tiny dining room chair in her small hand; the toothpick-size legs of the chair were in her other.

"Broke!" Emily announced importantly. "Uh-oh! Broke."

"Sounds like there's a lot of action going on in here."
Ryan walked into his daughter's room to see Alexa running
back and forth between the two constantly in-motion toddlers. He gazed around the room. "Where's Kelsey?"

Alexa ordered herself to remain calm. It wasn't easy. After all, she was currently engaged in aiding and abetting the
crime of trespassing. More unnerving still, her adversary
looked particularly strong and formidable this morning,
dressed as he was in a black shirt and black jeans. She decided that Ryan needed only a black cape and fangs to
achieve the dark menace of Dracula.

Alexa took a deep breath. "Kelsey is taking Dylan on a
tour of the house and grounds, riding him on her lap in the
wheelchair." She flinched at the blatant lie. The child riding on Kelsey's lap was her little brother, Kyle, today playing the role of Dylan, the third triplet. Melissa was
accompanying the pair on the house tour.

Ryan smiled, unaware of the deception. "Kelsey told me
you were going to bring the triplets to visit this morning. She
was intrigued by the idea of triplets. She couldn't wait to see
them. When I told her you were a triplet yourself, she was
awed."

"I remember that you used to refer to Ben, Carrie and me
as littermates," Alexa said bitingly. She cast a nervous eye
toward the door, silently willing Kelsey and Melissa not to
return with the *faux* Dylan.

"I was just kidding. You knew that, Alexa."

"You do have a talent for making a joke out of everything." Her tone was not admiring. "It's proven to be very
lucrative for you."

"That's true," he said flatly. "I joke about everything
and get paid for it."

And the more interested and involved he was in anyone or
anything, the more flippant he became. He'd always considered that his greatest asset. Now, staring at Alexa's wary
guarded face, he wondered if his cool, nothing-matters at-

titude wasn't also his worst fault. He wondered if it hadn't cost him far more than he had gained.

Such as the way Alexa was looking at him. There had been a time when she'd gazed at him with her light blue eyes glowing with warmth and love. Ryan felt a stab of pain. He'd suppressed that memory, just as he had suppressed so many others of Alexa. But since she had reappeared in his life, it was becoming impossible to keep those memories and feelings blocked. He was flooded by them and was fast reaching the point where he could think of nothing else. If she only knew how impatiently he'd been waiting for her to arrive this morning, pacing the floor of his studio like one possessed.

He realized that he was staring at Alexa like a glassy-eyed drunk. She was focused solely on retrieving a miniature plastic cake from little Emily's mouth. He could slip from the room and no one would even notice. Or care.

But Ryan made no move to leave. The urge to stay with Alexa, to reconnect with her, was too overpowering.

"I remember right after you told me you were a triplet, you said that your mother was a twin," Ryan said. "A little while later, you sprang the news that every woman on your mother's side of the family has given birth to twins or triplets, all the way back to your great-grandmother. Some genetic thing about multiple eggs being released simultaneously. I was fascinated."

"Fascinated? I thought you were appalled. I worried that you might work us into some kind of bizarre freaks-of-nature storyline in your strip." Alexa hoped she sounded suitably blasé. This was no time for a discussion on reproduction! She had to get Ryan Cassidy out of here and back to the confines of his studio. *Now!*

"Down right now!" demanded Franklin. When Alexa didn't move fast enough to suit him, he took matters into his own hands, slipping off the horse and crashing to the ground. Both Ryan and Alexa ran to him, but the little boy picked himself up and toddled away, none the worse for his landing.

"Whew! He's tough!" Ryan said admiringly. "When Kelsey would fall at that age, she would scream to high heaven." He smiled at the reminiscence and at the two busy toddlers making themselves at home in Kelsey's room. "So these are Carrie's triplets?" He wanted Alexa to smile with him, at him. "I remember them as infants, but—"

"Well, that was a long time ago," Alexa cut in. There was no answering smile for Ryan. "They've changed a great deal since then."

She doubted, however, that he would buy the notion that the "Dylan" currently visiting this house had also changed his hair and eye color and skin tone from the baby Dylan Ryan had seen only a few times two years ago.

After their quarrel yesterday, she had been counting on Ryan to keep away while she and the little ones were here. It was the only way for this Kyle-smuggling scheme to work, for as a set of triplets, Franklin, Emily and Kyle were sorely suspect. Emily and Franklin, like their real brother Dylan, were fair-skinned, blond and blue-eyed. They were also six months older than Kyle, who was shorter and slighter, had hair as black as Melissa's, big dark brown eyes and an olive complexion.

"Did you tell Carrie where you were taking them?" Ryan asked, watching Franklin and Emily head for a low shelf where a menagerie of stuffed animals perched. He wanted to keep the conversation flowing, and the children were a neutral, natural topic.

"Of course I told her. Did you think I'd kidnapped them? I often take the children on outings so it was no big deal," Alexa replied coolly.

She wasn't as cool as she sounded. Though she'd told Carrie about the visiting ban and the triplets' part to thwart it, she hadn't revealed the identity of the people involved. The mention of Ryan Cassidy ignited Carrie's wrath as well as Ben's; neither had forgiven him for his treatment of their sister.

Bringing Emily and Franklin here under false pretenses was probably a harebrained scheme, but Alexa thought of Kelsey's joyous expression at the sight of little Kyle, of the genuine affection the two displayed for each other.

And Ryan wanted to deny those poor children contact with each other! Alexa shot him a glare, a flame of righteous anger burning within her. But she was also very, very nervous. She had to get Ryan out of here and back to his studio before Kelsey and Kyle returned to the room! An argument seemed the perfect solution. And since the threat of the Tremaines seemed to inflame him, it was the perfect vehicle.

"I talked to my brother-in-law Tyler last night about going to court over that contract," she said. "Tyler said he would use every Tremaine resource available to back me up."

Actually, he'd said no such thing because the conversation hadn't taken place. What a liar she was becoming! A wave of shame washed over her. Being around Ryan was becoming detrimental to her character.

She stole a quick glance at him. He was watching her, his arms folded, his expression enigmatic. "There isn't going to be any court fight, Alexa," he said quietly. "I think you know that as well as I do."

Alexa began to panic. Why wasn't he tearing into her? This was not the time for him to turn reasonable! She tried again to stoke the fires of resentment. "So I scared you off, huh? I guess you don't dare cross the Tremaines in any way, not with their chain of bookstores being one of the largest and fastest-growing. You want to stay on their good side so they'll continue to stock your books."

Ryan cocked his head. He was determined not to further poison the atmosphere between them by quarreling with her again, but she was baiting him, there could be no doubt about that. Why? He stared at her flushed cheeks, her pale blue eyes that glittered with challenge.

Tentatively he sidestepped the gauntlet she'd thrown down. "I doubt that the Tremaines would ban my books from their chain, particularly not for—"

"They would," Alexa insisted. "One word from my sister Carrie—and she'd say it on my behalf—and your books would be gone from the Tremaine bookshelves overnight. Just like that." She snapped her fingers to dramatize her point. "You need *them* much more than they need *you*."

Because she was so obviously determined to start a fight with him, paradoxically, Ryan could not summon a lick of anger. His curiosity was roused instead. "Your point being that cartoonists with editions of their collected comic strips are a dime a dozen?" he drawled dryly.

"More like a penny a dozen," Alexa retorted.

"Horsie, ride!" Franklin demanded, back by the horse again. This time Emily chimed in her request. "Me too ride!"

Ryan and Alexa automatically headed for the horse. He picked up Franklin, she lifted Emily. In a moment, both children were seated on the carousel horse. And Alexa was only inches away from Ryan, who towered over her, tall and dark and heart-stoppingly virile.

For a moment, Alexa was afraid that her heart really had stopped. Then it seemed to start again, beating way too fast and poundingly loud. Alexa had to remind herself to breathe. He was so close, too close, and she could feel the heat emanating from his hard frame. With every gulp of air, she inhaled his musky male scent. Her mind was whirling, her thoughts jumbled and tumbling like pieces in a kaleidoscope.

Ryan gazed down at her, his eyes fastening on her seductively shaped mouth, as memories overwhelmed him. He remembered everything, the feel of her warm soft lips open under his, the erotic play of her tongue deep in his mouth. He remembered long, lazy hours in bed as she kissed her way down his body, his fingers threading through her thick mass of blond hair while that sultry mouth of hers closed over him, inciting his passion to a riotous level he'd never reached before or since her presence in his life.

Compulsively he reached for her, gripping her shoulders with his hands. She felt warm and strong, yet small and soft, and unable to stop himself, he began a slow, gentle massage with his long fingers. "Alexa, I don't want us to be enemies," he said raspily.

"Well, we are," she said, her voice soft and husky, her tone completely belying the content of her words.

The sound of that feminine huskiness had a startlingly sensual effect on Ryan. He felt a sharp thrust swell his loins and he breathed deeply, trying to control his reaction to her sexy voice and irresistible mouth. But the need to touch her, to be even closer to her, was a craving too compelling to resist.

Alexa stared up at him, her pale eyes connecting with his dark ones. The hungry intensity in his gaze wasn't masked, and she read it for what it was. Her whole body tightened with the sexual tension stretching between them. She felt shaky and breathless and weak. And she hated herself for it, hated him for reducing her to such a state.

"Get away from me, you snake," she said in a taut low voice. She jerked away from him and moved swiftly to the other side of the horse, so that it and the children were between them, a protective barricade against her own traitorous impulses. For a moment she forgot about Kelsey and little Kyle and her mission to keep their visit a secret. She forgot about everything but the pain and rage this man had caused her.

"Aren't you supposed to be working?" She glared at him while Franklin and Emily shrieked and bounced on the horse between them. "What about your famous comic strip? Don't you spend time on it anymore, or do you just fax in junk at the last minute without putting any thought into the story whatsoever?"

"Oh, I fax in junk moments before my deadline, of course."

Alexa didn't smile at the joke. She refused to be amused.

"Actually, I'm ahead of myself with the strip," Ryan continued. "I know you don't read *Howe, Ware & Wenn* but—"

"Howe, Ware & Wenn," Alexa scornfully repeated. "The title is so affected, so contrived. I guess you thought it was a cutesy play on words but the effect is just plain irritating."

"Yeah, that's exactly what I was aiming for—a cutesy but irritating play on words." Ryan's tone was as bland as his expression. If she was refusing to be amused, he was refusing to get annoyed.

Which greatly annoyed Alexa. She gave up trying to insult his work, as that route had led nowhere. "Don't you have anything better to do than to hang around and—and harass me?"

"You're not working, either," he pointed out. "In fact, your patient is helping you baby-sit." He smiled crookedly. "And it's a good thing. Keeping up with these two little dynamos is a nonstop job. I can't imagine adding a third!"

"No one is asking you to. Now get out!"

"You're throwing me out of my daughter's room, which happens to be in my own house?" He studied her intently. "You're hell-bent on provoking me, aren't you, Alexa? Why?"

The color in cheeks heightened. "So you'll go storming out of here and barricade yourself in your studio, of course." That was certainly the truth. "Since you seemed to be missing all my clues, I'll have to be even more explicit. I want you to go away and leave me alone."

"You don't like me very much, do you?" He was doing it again, playing it cool, joking and glib, while ignoring the pain lacerating him.

"You flatter yourself, Ryan. Actually, I don't like you at all."

Franklin chose that moment to dismount from the horse, grabbing on to Ryan and trying to use him as a human ladder to climb down from the horse to the floor.

Ryan was grateful for the distraction. Alexa's words, harsh and cold, were echoing in his ears, and he could think of no flip quip to come back with. He turned his attention to Franklin and managed to hold on to the wriggling child without dropping him, setting him safely on his feet.

Franklin ran toward the door, pausing to look back at Ryan. "C'mon," he ordered. "Go with Franklin."

"I think he wants to find his brother," Ryan said, amused by the general-to-private tone the toddler had adopted. It was clear in Franklin's mind who was in charge here. "I'll take him to find Kelsey and—"

"No!" Alexa cried. "You can't!"

Disaster loomed if he found the false Dylan. Ryan was not stupid. One look at Kyle, coupled with Melissa's presence, and Ryan would know the little boy wasn't one of Carrie's children. It would not take a great leap of imagination to figure out Kyle's true identity. Alexa imagined the bitter Ryan-Melissa confrontation that would follow the discovery of the deception and shuddered.

"I—I want Franklin to stay here where I can watch him," she insisted.

"You don't trust me with your nephew?" Ryan was stung by the thought.

Alexa accepted his misinterpretation as a gift from the gods. "That's right, I don't trust you with him," she snapped. "What if you get bored or distracted and forget about him? There are a hundred ways for a baby to get hurt in this place. He could fall over the railing or into the pool or—"

"I would hardly *forget* that I was looking after a child," Ryan gritted.

"Why not? After all, you forgot to mention to me that you were a father. If you could forget to mention the existence of your own child—"

"I didn't forget to tell you about Kelsey!"

"Oh, yes, that's right. You deliberately chose to conceal her existence from me. Lying by omission, I believe it's called. And it's just as reprehensible and deceptive as actively telling a lie."

"Go with Franklin!" Franklin raised his voice to match the volume of the adults, also managing to sound just as forceful and indignant.

Spontaneously, involuntarily, Ryan and Alexa both broke into grins at the sight and sound of the two-year-old dictator who clearly felt he was their equal, if not their boss. They glanced from Franklin to each other, humor and warmth shining in their eyes.

Ryan felt the ground tilt under his feet; there was a roaring in his ears. He was aware that the sweetness and love reflected in her expression was directed toward her small nephew, but it struck a chord deep within him. He remembered when she used to look at him that way—her face soft with love, her eyes glowing with affection—back in the days when she loved him. When they had been lovers. . . .

"Alexa," he said hoarsely. At this moment, he felt desperate to end the hostility between them.

Alexa sensed it and was thoroughly alarmed. If there was one thing she didn't dare do at this risky moment in time, it was to call a cease-fire. It was definitely time to bring in the heavy artillery.

She glowered at him, all traces of warmth gone. "Tell me, Ryan, did you remember to tell your *fiancée* that you have a daughter? Or have you decided to keep your child a secret from her, too?"

Five

    "My fiancée?" Ryan echoed.

    "I heard you're getting married," Alexa said tightly. The shaft of pain that stabbed her was almost physical in its intensity, but she bravely ignored it.

    "You did?" He stared at her. "From who?"

    Damn, she was back on the defensive! Alexa frowned. Bringing Melissa into the conversation—argument, whatever it was they were having—seemed foolhardy. He'd already accused her of being in *cahoots* with his ex.

    "Uh, Gloria mentioned it," Alexa said, not meeting his eyes. She made a mental apology to the older woman whom she'd now used twice as the source of confidential information. As a liar, she wasn't proving to be very original.

    "Gloria," repeated Ryan. "Well, she does speak what's on her mind...to whoever happens to be around to listen. Did she happen to tell you who it is I'm marrying?"

    He would be interested in knowing that himself. Where on earth had Gloria gotten the idea that he was engaged to be married? He racked his brains, trying to figure out who and what had brought Gloria to this conclusion. And when.

"I didn't bother to ask," Alexa snapped. "I have better things to do than to stand around and pump Gloria for personal information about you, although if I knew the name of the woman, I would send her a sympathy card, that's for sure."

"A sympathy card because she's marrying me?" Ryan's lips twitched, his dark eyes gleaming. "Well, Hallmark does seem to have a card for every occasion. I suppose they might have one that offers 'Deepest Sympathy on Your Choice of Mate.'" He smiled, inviting her to smile with him.

She didn't. "Isn't there anything that isn't a joke to you, Ryan? You even find humor in infidelity and betrayal and—"

"There are plenty of people who look only at the dark, intense side of every issue," Ryan cut in quickly. She was hitting perilously close to his own newly acknowledged insights. He felt troubled and defensive. "I just don't see what's so bad about viewing the craziness in this world from a different angle. From a humorous perspective."

"I'm not talking about your comic strip, I'm talking about you personally. You use humor to distance yourself."

"Well, you're using anger to distance yourself from me. You've been trying your best to infuriate me this morning. And I don't understand why."

"Poor misunderstood Ryan! All you want to do is to bury the hatchet and be friends. Is that the story you're trying to sell this time around?" Alexa folded her arms and rolled her eyes heavenward. "Well, if I'm stupid enough to buy that one, I deserve to have someone sell me an oceanfront condo in Nebraska."

"I'm not trying to sell you anything, Alexa. I simply want to—"

"This is a regular pattern with you, isn't it, Ryan?" Her voice was as accusatory as an avid prosecutor grilling a guilty defendant. "You're one of those despicable jerks incapable of commitment. You start cheating as soon as a woman gets too close. I'm speaking as an expert witness in your case. You and I got too close for your comfort, so you dumped me and immediately started running around with a whole battalion of women. And now you're engaged and marriage is looming, so you're looking to cheat again. This time *with* me!"

"I am not cheating—"

"Maybe not yet, but you're willing and ready!" Her light blue eyes burned with fury. "I saw the way you looked at me today, and I know what it means. We had a very intimate relationship for eight months and I recognize all your signals, Ryan."

"Well, I recognize yours too, honey," Ryan drawled. "And though you keep saying how much you want to be my enemy, you're sending an entirely different message nonverbally."

Frustration coursed through him. Their words always seemed to get in the way, whether two years ago or today. Either they said too much or not enough or all the wrong things. Ryan felt an unruly urge to yank her against him and indulge in some direct nonverbal communication. They communicated very well on that level; they always had.

"I am not!" Alexa was seething. His arrogance was intolerable. "You're definitely my enemy, and I wouldn't have it any other way. And—and even if you weren't, I am not the kind of woman who sneaks around with another woman's man!"

"This whole argument is ridiculous!" Ryan exclaimed. "Not to mention irrelevant because there is no—"

"Down! Want down right now!" Emily shouted imperiously.

There could be no ignoring that command. Ryan automatically reached for the little girl, lifting her off the wooden horse and setting her on her feet. "Here you go, little lady."

Emily looked up at him, those enormous blue eyes of hers puzzled. "Where I go?" she asked, puzzled.

Ryan was amused by her confusion. "I guess telling her it's a figure of speech isn't going to make things any clearer."

"Children are very literal at that age," Alexa said stiffly.

It was hard to stay focused on their argument with two lively toddlers distracting them.

"They sure are." Ryan watched Emily head back to the pile of stuffed animals she and her brother had thrown from the shelf. "She reminds me of Kelsey at that age. So bright and cute, running around, always on the move."

And then his smile abruptly faded and his face darkened with grief.

Alexa knew he was thinking of Kelsey today, still bright and cute, but unable to move the way she used to. Compassion washed over her, diluting her anger. She had to restrain herself from reaching out to him, to try to comfort him. She had always been attuned to Ryan, reactive to his moods and his needs. She was *too* attuned to him, even now, she thought resentfully. Ryan Cassidy could play her as skillfully as a master fiddler plucked the strings of his instrument.

"Alexa, will Kelsey ever run again?" Ryan's eyes were fixed on Emily and Franklin, who'd forgotten his demand to leave the room and had joined his sister amid the collection of animals. The ease with which they raced around, climbing and jumping, contrasted painfully with his images of Kelsey, trying so hard that sweat beaded on her forehead when she inched her way out of the bed and into the wheelchair.

"Will she ever be able to move around again without concentrating and working on each and every small motion? What if she is permanently paralyzed, Alexa? What if she can never take another step without braces and crutches or canes?"

"Then she'll learn to accept it and go on with her life," Alexa said quietly. "There is much more to Kelsey than a pair of legs, you know. There's certainly more to life than being able to run and jump. And there is no reason why she can't have a full wonderful life. Unless, of course, she is made to believe she is useless or not as good as she was before. That is the insurmountable handicap, and it's imposed by those who can't see beyond physical limitations and who don't bother to consider personality and character and all the other things that make a person unique."

"I guess you've given that speech to the parents of every kid you've ever worked with," Ryan said, sounding weary and dispirited.

"I mean every word of it. If a child is crippled psychologically, the effects can be more damaging than a physical impediment. For example, your fights with Melissa and the way Kelsey has learned to manipulate the hostility between you is going to hurt her future relationships far more than having to walk with braces ever would."

"Now that's what I call an underhanded attack." Ryan flared. "Bushwhacking me with Melissa under the guise of concern for Kelsey."

"I'm very concerned for Kelsey. And I'm interested in her total well-being, not just the nerves and muscles in her legs."

"Well, so am I!"

"And you don't consider banning her little brother from your property and threatening her mother with a custody fight as being detrimental to Kelsey's emotional health?" demanded Alexa.

"I want what's best for my daughter and—"

"No, you don't. You want things the way you want them for your own selfish reasons. Whether it happens to be the best—or the worst—for anyone else is totally irrelevant to you."

The insult burned him like acid. "That is both untrue and unfair."

Alexa was undaunted. "You're extremely adept at rearranging reality to suit your own purposes, Ryan. Maybe it comes from creating that comic-strip world of yours and having total control over it."

She took a deep breath and pressed on. She couldn't seem to stop herself. "I know because I personally experienced one of your 'it's for the best' rationalizations. According to you, it was 'for the best' that we not see each other anymore. Well, that wasn't what was best for me, but you wouldn't even listen to my side. I was banished from your life, and I was also supposed to believe that you were acting in my best interest so you wouldn't have to deal with the pain you'd inflicted. I loved you so much and—"

She broke off, horrified by her outburst. How, why, had she ever said that? She couldn't believe she'd done it! "Of—of course, that's all ancient history now." Aghast and embarrassed, she was talking more to herself than to him. "None of it matters anymore."

Ryan was silent. The things she'd said whirled through his brain. His perceptions shifted crazily, and suddenly he saw himself through her eyes. He didn't like the image presented, not at all. Suddenly things that had made perfect sense from his point of view seemed heartless and cold from hers.

"The person you've described—arrogant and selfish and manipulative—that isn't me," Ryan protested. His intense dark eyes sought hers.

"Oh, I'm sure you can produce a whole drawerful of testimonials extolling you as a stellar human being." Alexa shrugged. "But I'd be willing to bet that you're not close to any of those people, that they only know you through the carefully limited exposure you've allowed them. Would anyone you know feel close enough to you or comfortable enough with your friendship to suggest that you just might be wrong sometimes? Aside from Melissa, of course, whom you'd never listen to anyway?"

Ryan thought of his wide circle of acquaintances. Alexa was right; he wasn't really close to any of them. Certainly none of them would ever challenge his intentions or decisions. Neither would his father or Gloria. As for Melissa, he figured that since she saw him as Evil Incarnate, he might as well disregard anything she said as prejudicial and vengeful.

But when Alexa Shaw stood before him and accused him of putting himself above his daughter's emotional well-being for his own selfish reasons, it packed a potent wallop. She had always been able to breach the wall he'd built around himself, to puncture his guard and slip beneath the layers of control and indifference that he had cultivated since he was a lonely, defenseless boy. It was Alexa's singular ability to reach him on an emotional level no one else had, combined with her wholehearted love for him, that had compelled him to drive her out of his life.

He'd had to! Early on, he had blamed all the loss and pain and rejection in his life on love and loving, and had pledged never to fall victim to its curse again. If that meant not taking the love Alexa had offered, even though he had craved it, so be it. He'd been at war with himself over her, but his darker cynical side had prevailed. He had put her out of his life.

He permitted himself to love his child only; he prided himself on being a caring, generous, loving father. And now Alexa was denying that.

"I think you're jealous of Kelsey's affection for her baby brother," Alexa pressed on relentlessly. For better or worse, they were in this argument and she wasn't going to meekly retreat. "You view Kyle as an advantage that Melissa has and uses against you to win Kelsey, but the truth is, that little boy is a person in his own right and your daughter genuinely loves him. All the dolls and toys and possessions you shower on her won't take the place of her brother, and you're deluding yourself if you think they will."

Ryan looked stricken. "Is that what you think?"

Could it possibly be true? He thought of his reasons for banning "Melissa's brat" from his house when he'd brought Kelsey home from the hospital ten days ago. In the light of Alexa's accusations they now seemed trivial and self-serving. He considered the irritation he felt every time Kelsey mentioned her little brother. He didn't want to hear about that kid who was such an important part of his daughter's life—a part that totally excluded him.

"When you try to keep Kelsey and Kyle apart, you're as cruel as that first stepmother of yours who made your father get rid of the dog you loved so much," Alexa said, eyeing him intently. She wondered if she had gone too far. Ryan looked as if he had been stabbed in the heart and was slowly bleeding to death.

"The last thing in the world I ever intended was to be cruel to my child," Ryan said thickly.

"Maybe you didn't do it deliberately," Alexa conceded. He looked so distressed that she was moved to offer some sort of comfort, some reassurance. "There hasn't been any irrevocable damage done yet, Ryan. You could—"

She was cut off in midsentence when the bedroom door opened and Melissa stepped inside with a cheerful, "Hi, we're back!"

Alexa froze. So did Melissa. The color seemed to drain from her face. "Oh, Ryan, I—I didn't know—I just arrived and I—I was looking for K-Kelsey. Um, it looks like she's not here. Have you seen her, Alexa?"

If Melissa was trying to play the innocent, her performance was on the low end of the credibility scale, Alexa thought gloomily. Rather, she looked the picture of guilt.

Ryan knew at once that something was amiss. Striding across the room, he stepped out into the hall and returned a moment later, pushing Kelsey in her wheelchair. Kyle—aka Dylan—was perched happily on her lap, munching on a cookie.

Kelsey looked from her mother to Alexa with wide scared eyes. Nevertheless, she managed a smile for her father and said blithely, "Hi, Daddy. This is Dylan, Alexa's nephew. He's a triplet."

Ryan stared at the little boy for a long minute. Then he glanced over at Emily and Franklin who were pelting each other with stuffed animals. "Hey, kids," he called. "Where's your brother? Where's Dylan?"

Emily dropped the teddy bear she was about to hurl and looked around the room. "Where Dylan?" she asked, as if suddenly recalling her brother's absence.

"Dylan not here," Franklin reminded her. He grinned mischievously. "Dylan take a nap!" Apparently that was a bit of riotous toddler humor, for Emily dissolved into shrieks of laughter. So did Franklin. They resumed their animal tossing, oblivious to the tension in the room.

"Gee, that's odd. They don't seem to recognize their own brother," Ryan remarked casually.

"That's because they're dumb," Kelsey said quickly. "*Real* dumb. They don't have any memory. Isn't that sad?"

"I don't think it's because they're stupid," Ryan replied. "They seem like bright children to me. I'm going to take a wild guess and say that this particular Dylan—" he touched the little boy's dark, silky hair "—isn't actually their brother Dylan."

"Yes he is, Daddy," Kelsey insisted.

It saddened Ryan that his daughter felt the need to lie to him—and to stick insistently with that lie, even when faced with overwhelming evidence disproving it. Worse was the painful acknowledgment that he had driven her to it. He glanced at Melissa who had picked up her little boy and was holding him protectively, then flicked his gaze to Alexa.

No, he couldn't blame this one on Melissa, Ryan admitted to himself. It occurred to him that he'd blamed Melissa for so many things over the years that it had become a habit with him. Somewhere along the way he had rendered himself blameless, and he had gotten away with it. Until now. His eyes met Alexa's. There would be no more self-deception to believe the lie with her around.

Emily's and Franklin's squeals of laughter were the only sounds in the room. Ryan gazed down at his daughter's defiant upturned face. "I know that's your brother Kyle, Kelsey," he said quietly. "I know you wanted to see him, and I'm sorry you had to lie about it. I was wrong to say he couldn't come here." He raised his eyes to Melissa. "You can bring him over every day. Work out a schedule around the physical therapy and tutoring."

Melissa was visibly stunned. She seemed to have been rendered mute, for she simply gaped at him without saying a word.

"Thanks, Daddy!" cried Kelsey exuberantly. She held open her arms for a hug. "You're the best!"

Ryan swooped down and picked her up, clutching her tight.

Alexa felt her eyes mist. The heartfelt father-and-daughter embrace touched her deeply. More than it should have, she admonished herself. She tried to steel herself against the warm waves of emotion sweeping through her.

"Thank you, Ryan," Melissa said uncertainly. She seemed unsure whether to trust what she'd just seen and heard. "What made you change your mind?"

"Alexa pointed out a few things I hadn't considered," Ryan said, looking over Kelsey's head. His dark gaze met and held Alexa's.

"Well, I'd love to know what she said," muttered Melissa, "and how she ever got you to listen to her. You don't listen to anybody, Ryan Cassidy."

Alexa tensed. Apparently Melissa wasn't ready to be a gracious winner. "I just explained—uh—the importance of the sibling bond," Alexa said quickly. "You know, the necessity of maintaining it during convalescence. That sort of thing."

She glanced purposefully at her watch. "Goodness, look at the time! I have to get Emily and Franklin back to their mother right away. Kelsey, I'll be back in a little while for a shortened session today, but tomorrow we're back to a full-time workout, okay?''

"Okay," Kelsey agreed happily.

Alexa scooped up the two children, balancing one on each hip, and fled from the room. She made it as far as the garish, grandiose vestibule when Ryan's voice halted her.

"Alexa, I'd like to talk to you."

Alexa looked up to see him walking down that movie-set staircase toward her.

"I left Kelsey upstairs with her mother and brother," he said. "Mind if I ride along with you and the children?"

"Oh, that wouldn't be a good idea," Alexa said quickly. "I'm meeting Carrie at the food court of a shopping mall a few miles down the road to drop off the kids, and then I'll just turn around and come right back here to work with Kelsey."

Alexa clutched the two squirming toddlers tighter against her. She didn't want to be alone with Ryan, and with only Emily and Franklin as chaperons she might as well be. She had already spent too much time in his presence this morning, and this inner wellspring of churning emotions was the direct result. She felt off balance and vulnerable. Ryan's capitulation in the Kyle issue had astonished her, and the warm scene with Kelsey afterward had stirred her far too much. She had to get away from him to regain her emotional equilibrium.

"I'd like to talk about Kelsey," Ryan said, resorting to the one hold that he had on her. The only hold, he acknowledged ruefully. Alexa took her profession and her patients very seriously. She could tell Ryan Cassidy, her former lover, to get lost but she would never fob off Ryan Cassidy, concerned parent.

Alexa stood still, severely conflicted. Did he really want to talk about Kelsey, or was this a manipulative move that had nothing to do with his daughter and everything to do with his cheating on his fiancée? This morning she had helped Kelsey by somehow convincing Ryan that he was wrong to keep little Kyle away. It would be a shame to close the door, communication-wise, if there was a chance to help her patient further. On the other hand . . .

Alexa was about to consider that other hand, when the front door opened and Gloria came inside accompanied by a tall statuesque thirtysomething redhead who was carrying an expensive leather attaché case.

"Look who's here, Ryan!" Gloria sang out cheerfully. "And she's all ready to discuss those wedding plans of yours." She turned to the redhead, beaming. "Of course, you'll be staying for lunch, won't you, Judy?"

"Oh, definitely," said Judy. "I'll be here all day." She winked at Ryan. "I might even stick around for dinner, too."

"I—really have to go," Alexa said, hurrying out the front door, which still stood ajar. Her face was hot and flushed, and she welcomed the feel of the the cool October breeze against her skin.

She had seen Ryan's fiancée. *The woman was here to discuss wedding plans!* Alexa was rocked by the waves of pain and jealousy that simultaneously ripped through her. She blinked back a rush of tears, gulping around the lump that was blocking her throat.

She reached her car and quickly settled first Emily and then Franklin in their car seats, adjusting straps and fastening buckles. She was horrified that she was so perilously close to crying.

Her tears were merely some kind of a reflex action, Alexa assured herself bracingly; they didn't mean anything. They certainly didn't mean that she was upset because Ryan was getting married. After all, she'd heard about his wedding plans yesterday from Melissa and she hadn't cried then.

The sight of his fiancée hadn't bothered her. No, not at all. It was just that her emotions were still heightened from the successful resolution of the Kelsey-Kyle visitation problem. That had to be it!

She was over Ryan Cassidy, Alexa reminded herself sternly. She'd been over him for a long time. She was not the type to carry a torch for any man, particularly one that stayed lighted for two long years.

"Alexa!" Ryan shouted. Alexa glanced toward the house and saw him coming toward her, his stride brisk and purposeful.

Alexa panicked. She couldn't deal with him right now! She might be over him completely but seeing him again, spending time with him ... *She had to get out of here!*

"I'll talk with you about Kelsey some other time," she called. "I'm really pressed for time right now." She hopped into her car and gunned the engine.

A glance into the rearview mirror saw him standing in the driveway, his hands in the pockets of his jeans, staring after her. He stayed there until her car pulled out of the long driveway and rounded the bend in the road, disappearing from sight.

Six

____

The bright lights of the convenience store and gas station faded from view as Alexa turned the corner and strode briskly through the wide parking lot, taking a shortcut back to her apartment building. It was a beautiful night for a walk, with a full moon and lots of stars in the sky and a pleasant breeze rustling her hair.

She was in a strange mood tonight, Alexa mused, staring up at the fast-moving lights of a plane jetting across the dark sky. She felt restless, lonely and bored. Usually she relished quiet evenings alone, reading or watching videos, but tonight she had felt the need for company, for some kind of action.

She'd tried calling some friends but had no luck finding a companion. All were currently involved in relationships and unavailable for a spur-of-the-moment girls' night out.

Even Carrie and Ben were unavailable tonight. Though Alexa and Carrie remained emotionally close as ever, they didn't see as much of each other since Carrie's marriage to

Tyler. A husband created a whole new set of priorities and demands. Although Alexa was happy for her sister, she did miss the freedom of dropping in on her at any given hour. Ben's answering machine had informed all callers that he was "out." Ben spent most of his evenings out. He had a frenetic social life and no intentions of curtailing it.

"And I have no social life whatsoever," Alexa said aloud. Suddenly that bothered her. There had been a time when she'd had a lively one, but after her ill-fated involvement with Ryan, she had withdrawn, seeking solitude not company. The entire concept of dating seemed insane, a process of auditioning candidates to fill a position in her life that she didn't want filled. She didn't want another lover, she never wanted to fall in love again. It was too dangerous, the potential for heartbreak too risky.

She'd stuck to her vow, turning down invitations, staying home rather than going out, tuning out her worried parents' entreaties that she was becoming too reclusive, refusing Ben's frequent offers to "fix her up with a great guy." She had focused her attention and energy on her career, earning a name for herself as one of the most effective children's physical therapists in the area.

For the past two years, that had been enough. But tonight, suddenly her life seemed limited and intolerably dull. If she didn't get out of her apartment, she feared she would literally climb the walls. Thus, her trip to the convenience store. Though the six-pack of diet soda and two magazines she'd purchased there hardly qualified as dire necessities, getting out of her apartment, even for a little while, had *definitely* been necessary.

Alexa approached her apartment building—regretting that her errand was already over, wondering whether or not to invent a new one—when the headlights of a car appeared behind her. She automatically edged out of its way, but the car pulled alongside of her.

"Have you lost your mind?" an angry voice called from the car, the irate question unmistakably directed to Alexa.

She caught a glimpse of the driver while simultaneously recognizing the voice. Ryan Cassidy. Her heart began to thud, beating fast and hard against her ribs.

"What in the hell are you doing, walking around alone at this time of night?" Ryan demanded, sounding even more incensed.

"It's only nine o'clock and I needed something from the store," Alexa said, striving to sound nonchalant. She felt anything but. Ryan was here. She actually had to remind herself to breathe.

She saw his eyes flicker over her, taking in her black leggings and the plaid flannel boxers she'd pulled over them, her red University of Maryland sweatshirt and sturdy running shoes. She found herself wishing she had on something more attractive and less functional and was promptly horrified by her wayward thoughts. Ryan Cassidy was getting married. There was no reason why she should even want to appear alluring to him!

"You own a car. Why didn't you drive? There is absolutely no reason why a woman should walk alone in this area at night," Ryan scolded. "It's dangerous, it's foolish, it's downright—"

"I thought about driving," Alexa broke into his tirade. "But with car-jacking being the latest fad, I decided I'd be better off walking. Around here, criminals are out for cars not pedestrians."

She cast a cursory glance at his car which she identified as a 1963 Corvette Stingray, its split-window coupe's design giving it a futuristic supersonic look. Ryan was an American classic-car collector; her brother-in-law Tyler was, too, so she'd learned a bit about that category simply through osmosis.

"*You're* the one taking the big risk, driving that collector's item over here," she warned. "What are you doing here, anyway? Where is your fiancée? I believe her name is...Judy?"

She picked up her pace, keeping her eyes fixed straight ahead.

"Get in the car, Alexa," Ryan said roughly. "Right now."

Defiance streaked through her. "No, thank you. I'd rather take my chances with a mugger than ride with you." She walked even faster, deliberately ignoring his car inching along behind her.

Ryan parked the jet-black Stingray in the lot adjacent to her apartment building and followed her inside, a beat-up vinyl folder tucked under his arm.

"The crime rate in this area is increasing and the neighborhood is deteriorating," he growled, trailing her up the stairs to her second-floor apartment. "Why do you stay here?"

"I live here," Alexa countered crossly. "That's why I stay. And no one asked you to endanger yourself by leaving your grand mansion and coming down here. Slumming, I guess you'd call it."

They had reached her door. Ryan was standing beside her, still wearing the black shirt and jeans he'd had on earlier, and he looked lithe and muscular, dark and dangerous. Intriguingly, sexually dangerous.

"Go away, Ryan," she said in a low, shaky voice. She fumbled with her key, her fingers trembling.

Ryan took the key from her and inserted it in the lock. "I'm not getting married, Alexa." He pushed open the door and moved swiftly inside, before she had the chance to stop him.

Alexa set her plastic sack on an end table with a forceful thud. "Did you forget that I saw your fiancée today, Ryan? I heard Gloria say that Judy was there to talk about the wedding plans. So don't insult me by trying to deny what I heard with my own ears."

"I figured you wouldn't believe me so I brought proof." Smiling grimly, Ryan opened the vinyl folder, pulling out several sheets of paper crisscrossed with thin blue lines and sectioned into a series of pen-and-ink drawings.

Alexa recognized the paper as the kind Ryan used to sketch his comic strip at double the size the cartoons would be when reproduced for the newspaper format.

"Judy and I spent the day working on drawing the wedding of two of our characters," Ryan explained. "If you had stayed another minute this morning, I would've introduced you to Judy Gold who is the creator of *Look Both Ways*. It's a comic strip, Alexa."

"I know what *Look Both Ways* is. Just because I don't read your strip doesn't mean I avoid the comic pages altogether," she said coolly, with an unmistakable air of dismissal.

Ryan, however, refused to be dismissed. "*Look Both Ways* is a very funny strip, and since Judy stays away from controversy and sticks to that family of lunatics she created, her strip is syndicated in more papers than mine. She's never been exiled to the editorial page, either," he added wryly.

He held out the pages to Alexa. "Look at these. If you're familiar with *Look Both Ways*, you'll recognize Judy's characters. They're very distinctive from mine, which are here, too."

Alexa glanced at the drawings and quickly looked away. She wasn't sure she wanted to see them because they might be exactly what Ryan claimed. And that would mean Ryan's relationship with Judy was professional, that he wasn't engaged to be married and she would have to deal with his presence here in her living room.

Her mind was awhirl with confusion, and she knew that wasn't good, either. Not with her emotions in flux as they'd been tonight. Not with the reckless, dangerous excitement beginning to build and churn within her.

"What does any of this have to do with me?" she asked, feigning disinterest.

Ryan gave her a penetrating stare that brought a hot flush to her cheeks. He laid the drawings on the coffee table in front of her blue-and-green flowered sofa.

"Judy lives in the D.C. area," he said quietly. "We met professionally a few years ago and decided it would be fun to collaborate on a crossover story someday. Last month Judy came up with a secondary character whom we agreed would be the perfect match for one of my characters. One of those matches made in hell that's funny only in a comic strip."

"Sounds like a description of our former relationship. Although ours fit the format of a horror novel even better."

"No, that was my relationship with Melissa," Ryan corrected dryly. "You and I were more Disneyesque. *Beauty and the Beast* comes to mind."

Alexa stared at him impassively. No smile, not even a twinkle in her eye. Ryan sighed. "Well, back to Judy. She and I decided it would be more interesting if our characters appeared in both strips, exactly as they appear in their own strips. So we've been collaborating on the storyline and the drawings, which will culminate in the wedding at the end of the year. Each strip will offer similar versions but a different perspective."

He held up one panel. "Here they are—the bride and groom."

Alexa looked at the drawing, peopled by characters of both strips and signed by Judy Gold and Ryan Cassidy. She glanced up at Ryan and for a moment their gazes locked and a searing current of sexual tension flowed between them.

"This comic-strip wedding is as close as I've come to marriage with Judy Gold who, by the way, happens to be the happily married mother of two."

"Lucky Judy," Alexa said with a false lightness. "A happy marriage, children, a very successful career—she is one of the few women who really do have it all. But I still don't see what any of this has to do with me."

Challenge glinted in Ryan's dark eyes. "You described yourself as the kind of woman who doesn't sneak around with another woman's man. Well, there is no other woman in my life, Alexa. You obviously misinterpreted what Gloria said about the wedding and Judy and—''

"Actually, it wasn't Gloria who told me you were getting married," Alexa interjected quickly.

"So you overheard a few things and jumped to that conclusion all on your own?''

"No! I didn't creep around your house, eavesdropping. I was told you were getting married, but not by Gloria.''

"And you were jealous as hell, Alexa." Ryan looked extremely pleased at the notion.

Alexa felt the telltale blush darken her cheeks. "I was not! I was just—I—''

"Alexa, it's all right," he said warmly.

He moved quickly to stand before her, so close that Alexa could feel the heat and vitality of his body, the urgency emanating from him. It evoked too many sensual memories and a host of barely suppressed images of the two of them.

For her own self-protection, she had to erect some barriers and do it fast, by either attacking or withdrawing. Since she felt so wired, so edgy, an invigorating quarrel appealed far more than quiet retreat. And what better way to resume hostilities than to bring up the one person in the world guaranteed to raise his ire?

"Don't you want to know who told me you were getting married?" she asked archly.

Ryan's hand reached out to touch the side of her cheek. "Is it relevant?''

Alexa stood stock-still. She felt branded by the imprint of his palm. When his fingers moved to curl around the nape of her neck and stroke with a sensual mastery, she swallowed a small gasp. It was definitely time to assert herself.

"I think it's very relevant, Ryan." She jerked away and faced him defiantly. "It was Melissa.''

Alexa watched in satisfaction as Ryan's eyes narrowed and his mouth tightened. She'd hit her target. She braced herself for the ensuing fight, drawing up all her reserves to carry her to victory. "I don't know if Melissa overheard a few things and jumped to conclusions or if you encouraged her to think it but—"

"Why would I encourage Melissa to think I was marrying Judy Gold?"

"She didn't say it was Judy. I jumped to *that* conclusion on my own. But Melissa is convinced that you're getting married in order to have a stay-at-home wife to gain custody of Kelsey."

Ryan scowled. "That sounds like Melissa. Paranoid. Hysterical. She—"

"I see her as a mother who is terrified of losing her child to a rich and well-connected man, one who's able to afford a barracuda lawyer that will accommodate his demands, fair or not."

He sighed. "I can see that Melissa has been successful in painting me as the heartless villain and that you've bought her story lock, stock and barrel."

"Naturally. After all, we're in cahoots with each other." Alexa waited for the explosion. Instead there was a long silence. She stole a curious glance at him. "I just admitted that Melissa and I are plotting against you. Aren't you going to erupt?"

"Like a volcano?" He smiled without mirth. "Hardly."

"I know you prefer to annihilate your targets in one of your deadly cartoons, but you're quite capable of blowing up like a volcano when your temper is really roused. I've experienced it."

"Yes, you're quite capable of rousing me. Not only my anger but all my emotions." Ryan shook his head wryly. His dark eyes seemed fixed at a point beyond her. "All those years I'd lived my life trying to keep myself anesthetized from feeling too much and succeeding damn well at it. And then I met you—an idealistic virgin who was optimistic and emotional and passionate, a warm loving woman who made me feel things and feel them deeply. It was too much. It scared the hell out of me and I cut you loose."

Alexa stared at him with round shocked eyes. "You dumped me because you were tired of me," she reminded him. "You wanted to be free to be with other women."

"Yes, that's what I said, didn't I? Well, I was lying, Alexa. To you and to myself. There hasn't been anyone else since you've been gone."

"Oh, give me a break, Ryan. Don't lie about something that can be disproved so easily. The local papers and magazines have printed plenty of pictures of you with your various women, living it up in the thick of the Washington social scene."

"I plead guilty to dating and having my picture taken. That doesn't mean I've bedded a different woman every night. The truth is I've practically lived like a monk these past two years."

Alexa laughed at that. An angry scornful laugh, devoid of humor. "And what monk goes to the most gossiped-about party of the year thrown by the notorious Luke Minteer himself, accompanied by a thirty-eight double-D, platinum blonde named Storm? Don't bother to deny it because my own brother saw you at that party, with that very person."

"If Ben had spoken to me that night instead of glaring daggers at me all evening, I would've introduced him to Storm—my former stepsister. She is exactly as you described, but I've known her since she was twelve. My feelings toward her are strictly brotherly and definitely not carnal."

Alexa's eyes widened with curiosity. "Is she the stepsister your father—er—married?"

"You know about that?" Ryan grimaced. "From Melissa, no doubt." He sighed. "No, Storm isn't my latest stepmother. That would be Summer. She was thirteen the year her mother Nadine married my dad. The little sister, Sky, was ten."

"Wait a minute! Sky, Summer, and Storm? You're making this up, Ryan Cassidy."

"I wish." Ryan shook his head. "No, not even I would create a tale as perverse as Dad taking off with his step-daughter. I was twenty when he married Nadine, and I considered her daughters little girls. Who could lust after young women you'd watched grow up? I assumed Dad felt that way as well—until he ran off with Summer two years ago."

Clearly he was still troubled by the match. Alexa felt a twinge of sympathy for him. "Well, she's not a little girl anymore," she offered. "If my math works out correctly, Summer is a year older than I am. She's not a child anymore, she's an adult, Ryan."

"Her age is almost irrelevant," Ryan growled. "Dad was a father figure to her for years, not to mention the fact that he was still married to her mother. Poor Nadine went ballistic, homicidal one day, suicidal the next. It was a terrible time."

"Two years ago," Alexa murmured thoughtfully. "We were seeing each other then but you never mentioned a word of it to me."

"I couldn't. At least that's what I told myself at the time. You were so sweet and wholesome. You and your devoted, intact family could be the poster clan for family values. Then there was my wacko stepfamily." He frowned. "The entire Dad-Summer mess enraged me, made me even more cynical than I already was. I had no faith in anyone or anything."

"Including me and our relationship?" Alexa guessed softly.

Ryan's dark eyes, blazing with intensity, met hers. "I know this sounds weird and unfair, but I partially blamed you for making me feel all the pain and fury Dad and Summer unleashed. I'd successfully managed to keep myself numb for years. I didn't feel my own pain, let alone someone else's. But you got to me, you broke through that wall I'd constructed. . . ." His voice trailed off.

Alexa and Ryan stared silently at each other.

"I hated that I felt so much emotion about anything, be it love or anger." After a few moments, Ryan picked up where he'd left off, his tone rueful. "It reminded me of being a powerless kid, and I wanted no reminders of that. Then there was Kelsey. I felt guilty that I hadn't told you about her, that I was missing visits with her because I was with you. But whenever I was with Kelsey, she was all caught up in the excitement of Melissa's baby, her brand-new little brother, Kyle. She talked about him and Melissa and Jack all the time. I felt alienated from her. Like I was losing my child. So what did I do?"

He shrugged and proceeded to answer his own question. "Following the vaunted Cassidy tradition, I made a bad situation even worse. I broke up with you, the one person who loved me and could've—"

"No," Alexa cut in vehemently. "I'm not buying this revisionist history of yours, Ryan. Maybe there is a grain of truth in it but you aren't telling the whole story. For instance, what about your decorator girlfriend? The one who turned your house into an interior designer's joke. You said that she—"

"Nadine—Dad's third wife, mother of Summer, got all that?—was the one who decorated my house. Nadine's— uh—new to the interior decorating business. And she's finding clients difficult to come by. One look at my place and you can guess why," he added dryly.

Alexa stared at him. It was all starting to make sense to her, and that alarmed her. *To understand all is to forgive all.* Wasn't that how the old adage went? And the prospect of understanding and forgiving Ryan for the hurt he'd caused her made Alexa feel vulnerable indeed. She'd constructed some self-protective walls of her own, and seeing Ryan as a calculating manipulator was a cornerstone in her defense.

"Why are you telling me all of this now? You must have some self-serving motive." She paused, seeking it. And then it struck her. That passionate kiss in the hall, those sizzling stares. "Is it part of some calculated plot of yours to get me into bed?" What else could he possibly want from her?

"Sweetheart, I—"

"Sweetheart?" Alexa echoed incredulously. When was the last time he'd called her 'sweetheart'? For that matter, when was the first time? Right now! It was proof enough for her.

"I'm right!" she cried indignantly. "Oh, I can't believe it took me this long to put it together. You haven't exactly been subtle tonight, Ryan. The signs are all there. This impromptu visit of yours, your eagerness to prove you're eligible and unattached, the candid revelations about your family, even your restraint about Melissa. You came here tonight for sex, and you'll say anything to make sure you get it."

Ryan groaned. "You're determined to see me in the worst possible light."

"But I'm right, aren't I?"

"I've—missed you, Alexa. I didn't realize how much until you came back into my life."

She arched her eyebrows. "Oh?"

Her patent disbelief was unnerving. Even worse was her cynicism, so at odds with the trusting, loving young woman he'd known before. He drew a deep, steadying breath. If only he could reach her.

"Alexa, there's more. Much more. It's as if I've been wrapped in some kind of shroud of denial. I didn't let myself acknowledge how empty—how *lifeless*—my life has been without you in it. I went through the motions of existing—eating, sleeping, working, even socializing—but there was no pleasure in any of it. I felt nothing. You were the only person who made me feel really alive. When I was with you, I was living not existing, feeling joy and anger and pain. And I couldn't handle it, Alexa. From the day my mother died I'd—"

"Ryan, it's not going to work, not this time." Alexa sighed wearily. "I know I always used to be susceptible to a sad story, and you've never been averse to using the traumas in your life to get what you wanted but now—''

"Is that what you think?" Ryan was appalled. "On the contrary, I never discuss my personal life with anybody. You're the only person I've ever confided in, Alexa."

"Oh, sure! Right. And Princess Di and Prince Charles lived happily ever after."

"I came here tonight to tell you I want you back, Alexa," Ryan said bluntly.

Alexa stared at him, saw the determination glittering in his dark eyes, his stance and body tension radiating his intent. Her heart lurched crazily and her legs were suddenly, unnervingly weak. She hated that he still had the power to shake her.

She remembered all the tears she had cried when he'd ended their relationship two years ago, how she had been tormented with the pain of losing him. She remembered all those nights when her body had ached with the emptiness of missing him. But he hadn't come back to her. He'd let her suffer through the breakup, without ever calling once to see how she was doing. His screwy family and their problems notwithstanding, he hadn't called her in two years and now he was here claiming to *want her back?*

A fierce anger began to surge through her body. "You want me back," she repeated mockingly. "You come waltzing in here, having ignored my existence for the past two years, to tell me that *you want me back.*"

Her rage was spiraling into a wild reckless force. "And how did you expect me to react to your announcement, Ryan? Was I supposed to swoon with ecstasy because you've decided *you want me back?* Did you imagine I'd throw myself into your arms and sigh, 'Oh, goody, *you want me back'*?"

Ryan stood very still, his eyes meeting hers. "I guess I'd hoped you would say that you wanted me back, too."

"Yes, your ego is massive enough for you to think I would!" Alexa was trembling with the force of her fury.

"You could look at it in a more positive light," Ryan suggested wryly. "That my ego is strong enough to admit I made a mistake by letting you go."

"Letting me go? That's putting it mildly. You kicked me out of your life!"

"I know," he admitted heavily. He remembered the night he'd done it, the terrible ambivalence that had gripped him as he convinced himself he was doing the right thing for both of them. He remembered her white shocked face as he spoke the words, he remembered how he'd deliberately hardened his heart and tramped down the instinct to take her into his arms and make everything all right between them.

He could do that now, Ryan thought, hope and determination bolstering him.

"Alexa, I want to make it all up to you," he said urgently. "I want to make up for everything, the pain I've caused you and the two years we've lost and all the—"

"I can't believe you thought you could walk back into my life after two years and expect to find me waiting patiently for you." Alexa was incensed. "Did you really believe we could just pick up where we left off *two years ago?*"

He didn't answer immediately; he appeared to be assessing her every word. "Are you saying that it's too late?" he asked slowly. "That you're involved with someone else?"

That such a possibility hadn't occurred to him before this very moment intensified her wrath with the same incendiary force as a blast of pure oxygen to a flame. Pride demanded that she say Yes!

"It's over between us, Ryan. It's been over for a long time. And—and of course there is someone else! Did you think I'd spent the past two years pining over you?" She certainly hadn't, Alexa assured herself. She hadn't, even though there had been no one else who'd filled her thoughts and her dreams.

"Who is it?" he demanded starkly.

"Are you asking who I'm involved with? You want a name?" Alexa gulped. She didn't have one to give him.

"Yes."

"Why? What's it to you? What difference could it possibly make?" She was caught in her own trap. Pressured to come up with a name, her mind seemed to have temporarily gone blank.

"Why don't you want to answer me?" Ryan countered.

"Because it's none of your business."

"I consider anything having to do with you my business, Alexa."

She drew in a quick, angry breath. "I'm horrified to hear it. Not that I believe you."

"No?" He caught her arm and turned her toward him.

"No." Desperately she tried to wrench her arm from his grip but Ryan held on fast, catching her other arm to hold her still in front of him.

"I haven't heard a word from you for the past two years. Now suddenly, you're not only interested in me again, you're overly possessive!" Sheer pride forced Alexa to meet his gaze instead of avoiding it, as she instinctively wished to do. "It doesn't make sense. Furthermore, I'd be an idiot to put faith in anything you do or say."

It was a harsh indictment. The realization that, from her point of view she was acting wisely, sent a twist of pain flashing through Ryan. How many times had he said one thing and meant another, done something completely at odds with what he really needed and wanted? It was a method of self-protection he'd adopted as a hurt lonely child, one which no longer served him well. He saw that now with startling clarity.

"Nothing in my life has ever made any sense," he said slowly. "Not until now, Alexa." His hands glided upward and clamped over her shoulders.

Alexa's heart took a breath-stopping leap. She'd made a major mistake, letting him get this close when she was in such a weird, unpredictable mood. She was much too affected by his raw virility, which set her senses reeling and called back too many memories of those rapturous times she had spent in his arms.

"Go away," she said shakily, sliding her hands up to his chest to push him away.

But somehow, she forgot to push. She felt his muscled warmth and went blank. She inhaled the intoxicating male muskiness of his skin and her whole body reacted to the stimulus of his touch. Her nipples tightened, demanding the touch of his hands, of his mouth; there was a throbbing, swollen emptiness between her legs that ached to be filled.

Her nearness was having a similar, mind-shattering effect on Ryan. They were so close, they were touching each other, and he was compelled to make the contact more intimate, more possessive. He began to smooth his hands up and down her arms in slow sensual strokes.

"I don't want to go," he said huskily, "and you don't want me to leave, Alexa." His lips nibbled along the sensitive curve of her neck, arousing a deliciously exciting response within her.

Alexa shivered as tight coils of desire deep inside her began to unwind with forceful urgency. Her lashes flickered and closed as his mouth continued its assault. She was aware that she was moving against him in a slow seductive rhythm, her body setting the tempo independently of her mind.

But her mind was weakening, too. Suddenly the sensual power Ryan had over her didn't seem quite so threatening because she could feel the hard male evidence of his own desire, and she had the satisfaction of knowing that she was the cause of it. The exciting realization of her own feminine power pleased her. Ryan wanted her. There could be no doubt about that.

And then his big hands slid under her sweatshirt, his palms gliding along the bare skin of her back, his fingers caressing the fine straight line of her spine. Alexa held her breath when he reached the cotton barrier of her bra, then emitted a soft whispery cry when he swiftly, deftly unfastened the clasp.

She stood on tiptoe, pressing against him, needing to feel the hard muscled heat of his body against hers, craving the strength of his arms wrapped tightly around her. Their mouths met and clung with hungry urgency, his tongue thrusting into the moist warmth of her mouth, her tongue teasing his, rubbing, then retreating.

A low growl escaped from Ryan's throat as he took control of the kiss, deepening it, probing her mouth with a devastating intimacy. He felt the quivering response of her body and arched her provocatively against him so they both could feel the sweet pleasure of her breasts pushing against his chest.

Vaguely it crossed Alexa's mind that she probably should resist—*definitely* should resist?—but it was all too engrossing, too exhilarating to stop. Ryan was her first and only lover, and being in love with him had been the deepest, most intense emotion she had ever known. Making love with him had been the wildest, most enthralling pleasure she had ever experienced, and right now her body was hungry to experience it all again.

"Tell me I can stay, Alexa," Ryan coaxed. His hands glided round to cup her bare breasts, his thumbs circling her nipples as they budded tightly under his touch.

Alexa's breath shuddered out as hot pleasure shimmered through her. She felt wildly alive, her every nerve ending tingling. She knew she should push him away, but denying him meant denying herself and she couldn't seem to do it.

"You want to stay with me?" She sounded dazed, even to her own ears. "Tonight?"

"Yes, yes," he breathed. His mouth took hers again in a deep hot kiss that sent frissons of pleasure ricocheting throughout her body.

Alexa could feel the steely strength of his muscles under her hands, could feel his bold arousal that matched the throbbing heated need within her. Would it really be so bad to sample the passion they'd once known? she wondered achingly. Just one more time?

Ryan lifted his mouth from hers and gazed deeply into her eyes.

"I don't know," she whispered, answering her own silent questions aloud. She moved out of his arms, stepping just out of his reach. "I just don't know."

"Give me a chance to convince you," he coaxed. He stretched out his arm to catch her hand and carefully twined his fingers with hers.

"You mean, give you a chance to seduce me," Alexa corrected. "This time, at least let's be honest with each other, Ryan." But she didn't pull her hand from his.

"If we're going to be honest, then let's admit that I don't have to seduce you. We're long past that point, Alexa."

His dark eyes glittered. He felt as if he were on fire with a desire so fierce, it bordered on violence. She was letting him hold her hand but he wanted more, much more. He wanted to feel her clinging to him, weak with wanting, he wanted to hear her moaning with ecstasy when he took her. *She couldn't send him away now!*

"Please, Alexa."

Seven

The raspy huskiness in Ryan's voice as he pleaded with her was a source of arousal in itself. Alexa glanced down at their linked hands, his long strong fingers interlaced with hers, and a shiver of pleasure streaked through her. Ryan was right. This was not a seduction of a naive innocent by a wicked smooth operator. She was definitely a consenting participant.

She was also trapped in a paradox. She had always believed that sex without love was not for her. Yet here she was, burning with passion for Ryan, a man she professed not to love. The urge to simply give in to this exhilarating desire and live for the moment—just this one time—was too compelling to resist.

Ryan pulled her back against him, positioning her intimately into the cradle of his body and locking his hands around her waist. "What are you thinking?"

His teeth nipped at her earlobe; his hands moved upward to cup her breasts through the soft cotton of her sweatshirt.

Her unclasped brassiere dangled against her skin, reminding her of their earlier intimacy—and how good his hands had felt on her bare flesh.

"I'm not thinking clearly, that's for sure," Alexa said thickly. She snuggled back against him, her eyelids drooping, heavy with passion. As if of their own volition, her hands covered his, pressing them against her breasts while her head lolled back against his shoulder. "I'm not thinking at all!"

Ryan laughed a little. "Maybe that's not such a bad thing, Alexa." He continued to fondle her until a tiny moan escaped from her lips.

"Maybe not." She sighed.

Never before had she experienced this wild blind need to succumb to the moment. Yet it seemed so right, so inevitable that she would experience such abandon with Ryan Cassidy. He had always been the one to unleash the passion that her disciplined well-controlled character held carefully in check. He was the only man who had ever reached her on that level.

Alexa turned to face him, her decision made. She wanted him, but she wasn't about to give him everything, not this time. Years before he'd had her body, heart and soul, and he had cavalierly walked away from her. Whatever his reasons, he had done it and not looked back. This time her heart and soul would remain safe in her own keeping. Tonight was strictly physical. It was important that she make that clear.

"I have to be honest with you, Ryan," Alexa whispered. "I want to make love with you but I—I don't love you anymore."

Ryan flinched. *I don't love you anymore.* The painful words echoed in his head but he couldn't bring himself to believe her. Though she was hesitant to say it now, she would give him her declaration of love tonight, he was certain of it. He just needed to be patient.

"Then I guess I'll have to take whatever you're willing to give me, Alexa."

Alexa was thrilled by his admission, suddenly giddy with the heady sense of her own power. *He would take whatever she was willing to give?* Alexa smiled. The girl who had been left crying her heart out over Ryan's rejection had evolved into a woman to be reckoned with.

She slid her hands over his hard muscular frame, pressing herself into the masculine planes of his body, reveling in the feel of him and his undeniable response to her. "As long as we both understand we're—"

He silenced her with a passionate kiss and Alexa responded with every fiber of her being. A tiny whimper of need escaped from her throat.

Ryan scooped her up in his arms and carried her to her bedroom. Alexa linked her arms around his neck and closed her eyes. She was aching with the sweet, violent pain of wanting him, but she wanted the sexual heat to burn faster, hotter, so that she had no time to reconsider. She wanted to act in the passion of the moment with no time-outs for anything deeper.

"Just this once, I don't want to think," she whispered urgently. "Make me stop thinking tonight, Ryan."

"No thinking," he agreed. "No recriminations or no regrets. Tonight there is just the two of us, right here, right now."

"Yes." She nuzzled his jawline, aroused by the feel of his abrasive skin there. "Just for tonight, just this once. No past or no future."

The bedroom was dark but neither bothered to switch on a light. Ryan set Alexa on her feet beside the bed and drew her in his arms. "I want you so much, Alexa," he murmured, gazing down her, his eyes hooded and dark with sensuality.

Swiftly, deftly, he divested her of her sweatshirt and bra, dropping them to the floor. Alexa watched his dark gaze linger on the soft white fullness of her breasts as his hands traced the lush feminine curves of her body.

His eyes met hers for a long moment. "You're so beautiful, Alexa." His voice resonated with desire, his gaze was warm with appreciation of her body.

Alexa basked in that warmth, feeling a syrupy languor spread through her that was just as potent as the sharp edgy excitement it displaced. When Ryan eased her onto the bed, she lay boneless and pliant under his caresses.

"I remember when we bought this bed," he remarked, flicking gaze over the double bed with its brass headboard and yellow-and-blue flowered quilt. "We went to that furniture outlet in Potomac Mills and picked it out the day after we'd slept together for the first time—in that little twin bed of yours."

"We hardly slept a wink that night," she remembered with a soft smile. "My old bed was small for one person, let alone two."

"Mmm, true. But as I remember, it wasn't really the bed's fault that we were awake all night. We had better things to do than to sleep." He tugged off his shirt and threw it over the side of the bed, then propped himself up on one elbow.

Alexa stared at him, drinking in the sight of his chest, which was tanned and corded with muscles and sprinkled with wiry, curling hair. "You were relentless that night," she breathed in a seductive whisper.

"You were, too." He gently traced the shape of her taut rosy nipples, first with his fingers, then with his lips. "You smashed the shy cringing virgin stereotype to smithereens. You were so sexy, so passionate..."

His voice trailed off as he laved one tight pink bud with his tongue. Trembling, Alexa clutched his head to her breast, letting the deliciously arousing sensations flow through her. She felt a sharp, visceral pang of desire as Ryan drew the sensitized nipple into the wet warmth of his mouth and began to suck gently.

Alexa couldn't hold back her moan of intense pleasure.

"You still are, Alexa," Ryan said huskily. "Sexy. Passionate. So very responsive. You're the sweetest, most open and honest lover that I—"

"All these compliments," Alexa interrupted, stretching languidly, her movements deliberately sensual and sinuous. Ryan's pupils dilated, signifying his intensifying arousal. She preened under his hot gaze.

"You're quite good at finding the right words, Ryan." Lucky for her, she wasn't about to take them to heart this time. She'd done that before, to her own folly. "But then, I guess you have to be, since words are your stock-in-trade. Along with your drawing skills, of course."

"I'm not just saying words, Alexa." Frustration warred with the wild need coursing through him. Though she wasn't distancing him physically, her emotional withdrawal bothered him greatly. "I really mean them."

"You don't mean anything you say," she said blithely. "And you never say what you mean. Those are direct quotes, from you. Remember that interview with—"

"Stop it, Alexa," he ordered raggedly. "I know what you're trying to do and it's not going to work. I won't let you shut me out while you try to play it cool. I won't let you hide behind a barrier of cynicism. Tonight nothing is going to come between us. We're together and there aren't going to be any games or any invisible walls keeping us apart."

"Well, that'll certainly be a first, won't it?" Alexa knew she was baiting him but she couldn't seem to stop herself.

"Before it was always me doing the distancing," Ryan agreed with a grave nod, surprising her. "That's why I knew exactly what you were doing."

"It really does take one to know one, I guess. But this is no time for soul-searching and intimate confessions," Alexa said lightly. She refused to take him seriously; she didn't dare. "Remember, no recriminations, no re—"

"Shut up, Alexa."

He took her mouth fiercely and kissed her until both were too breathless to speak at all. They resumed their intimate explorations of each other, their passion burning wilder and hotter with every new sensual foray.

Alexa felt the hard strength of his fingers smooth over the length of her rib cage, then dip beneath the waistband of her leggings to circle the small hollow of her navel. She closed her eyes, shivering with anticipation as he explored the curve of her hip and then lightly, tantalizingly touched the softness between her thighs with his fingertips.

Her head spun as the excruciating excitement built within her. Her fingers clenched violently into the muscular hardness of his shoulders. "Ryan, I—I feel like I'm going out of my mind," she confessed as she tugged at the buckle of his belt. "I can't wait. I need you so."

"I know, baby. I know. It's the same for me."

It had always been this way when they'd made love, Alexa thought dizzily. All her senses heightened and filled. The sexy sounds they made...the sight of their bodies, contrasting and complementing...the taste and feel of him...his own masculine aroma, a seductive scent of soap and after-shave and clean male sweat...

Just one more time, she wanted to experience everything, all of him again. *Just this once...*

Ryan's mouth closed over one aching nipple and a knot of tension, so intense it bordered on pain, tightened between her legs, making her want to plead for release. The fire radiated from the intimate secret core of her, and Alexa arched into him, undulating her hips, desperate to satisfy her aching emptiness.

Her unabashed need sent another surge of heat through Ryan. He stripped the rest of her clothing from her, then threw off his own clothes before he swiftly rejoined her on the bed. Alexa welcomed him eagerly, and for one long incredibly sweet moment, they embraced, lying together naked, breast-to-chest, stomach-to-stomach, thigh-to-thigh. Loin-to-loin.

"It feels so good to hold you like this." Ryan groaned with pleasure. "It's as if we've never been apart. We shouldn't have been apart, Alexa. I was so wrong to—"

"We agreed not to get into that," Alexa whispered, laying her fingers lightly over his lips.

Ryan was eager to please her. Further talk would have to wait.

He slipped his hand between her legs, his long fingers stroking the silken skin of her inner thighs, then tangling in the downy softness to probe the moist feminine folds within.

Alexa whimpered, surrendering to the powerfully pleasurable sensations his caressing fingers evoked. Time and reason spun away with incredible, dizzying speed as the blazing internal waves crested, then suddenly erupted in flash fire of rapturous heat.

For long moments afterward, tiny shock waves kept shimmering through her. Blushing, Alexa hid her face against Ryan's chest, her eyes squeezed tightly shut as he held her, tenderly stroking her hair. It had happened so fast! She was both embarrassed and disconcerted. He'd barely touched her and she had exploded like a rocket off its launching pad. Her body had given him incontrovertible evidence of his potent effect on her, his sexual power over her.

It was knowledge that she didn't want him to have; she didn't like knowing it herself. If he were to gloat, to boast about his fantastic technique and the speed to which she'd succumbed to it ... Alexa stiffened, bracing for the worst.

"Alexa?" Ryan murmured softly.

Alexa opened her eyes to find him watching her expectantly. She felt the tension pulsing through him and sensed his iron control was ready to snap.

"Now, Alexa?" was all he said, for which she was infinitely grateful.

She nodded and he reached to the floor for his jeans, pulling out a foil packet from the pocket. Alexa's blush deepened. He'd come prepared. She didn't even want to think of the ramifications of that! "Were you so very sure of me, or are you always equipped for a possible—"

"Don't," he ordered, preparing himself, then lowering his full weight upon her. "I won't rise to the bait so don't cast it."

"You don't want to fight with me?" she mocked. But she wrapped her arms around him, arching her hips intimately to his. She felt him against her, hard and hot and needful.

"God, no," Ryan groaned. He mastered her body slowly and completely, surging into her, murmuring loving words and sexy words, in turn tender and exciting, as they broke the dark silence.

Alexa shuddered at the impact of his penetration and he stilled, allowing them both to adjust to the intimate joining. She tightened her arms and legs around him, bringing him even closer, his heavy strength filling her and satisfying the deep, empty ache within her.

"It's been so long," she whispered, slightly delirious with the profound emotions and sensations rippling through her.

"Too long. But we're together at last, my sweet baby." Ryan groaned blissfully against her lips. Sheathed deeply in her welcoming warmth, he felt a marvelous sense of completion. How had he managed to live without this, without her? Never again would he let her go. That was his last coherent thought as he was swept with her into the stormy vortex of their passion.

They moved together, the erotic rhythm of their movements growing faster and harder, the pulsing tension winding tighter, until the coil of spiraling passion snapped. Wild waves of intense shuddering pleasure crashed through them as their bodies convulsed in simultaneous ecstasy.

They lay together quietly for a long time afterward, bathed in the warm, languorous glow of fulfillment. It was Ryan who finally broke the relaxed, contented silence.

"There is a mawkish quote I savaged in one of my strips awhile back—it goes something like: 'This is the first day of the rest of your life.'" His voice was husky, filled with indulgent humor. "Have you heard it?"

"Of course. It's also a highly marketed quote. I've seen it on everything from pillows to posters to pieces of shellacked wood sold in turnpike rest stops. I imagine you offended quite a few people by trashing it."

"Oh, I did get complaints. Not the usual volume of hate mail, but I ticked off a goodly number of folks by mocking their credo."

"And that made you happy, I'm sure." She cuddled closer, her head resting on his shoulder, one leg tucked between his. "Nothing excites you more than riling people."

"Well, not exactly." He kissed the top of her head. "You top the list of what excites me. Riling people is second."

"But a very close second, hmm?" Her lips curved into a smile but she didn't open her eyes. She felt peaceful, drowsy and well sated, and wanted to do nothing more than fall asleep in Ryan's arms.

"Can't compare," Ryan disputed. He stroked her long, thick blond hair with gentle hands. "Anyway, now I'm sort of sorry I mocked that quote because I finally get it. It's the way I feel now, about us. That this is the first day of—"

"No, please! No platitudes, especially not mawkish ones!" Playfully she laid her fingers over his lips. "Your fans would be absolutely crushed. Lucky for you, I won't breathe a word of your lapse into sentimentality. Unless you were being ironic. Or satirical. In that case—"

"Alexa, this is no time for joking around," he cut in, dismayed.

Her lighthearted mood did not match his own. He felt intense and earnest and deeply committed. Her attitude was in striking contrast. Dry and teasing... rather pleasantly detached. The realization shook him, driving him to greater urgency. "Sweetheart, I'm trying to tell you how much I—"

"You don't have to tell me anything, Ryan." It was Alexa's turn to interrupt. Her eyelids had snapped open and she was looking at him warily. "There's no need to say a thing."

"No need? Of course there is, Alexa. We're finally back together."

"No." Alexa abruptly sat up. "We're not back together, Ryan."

His dark eyes narrowed to glittering slits. "We just made love, Alexa. I'm lying here in bed with you. We are most definitely back together."

"I guess that depends on how you want to define 'back together,'" she said lightly, edging away from him. She grabbed the edge of the sheet and pulled it to her throat, unnervingly aware of her nakedness. She was in a very vulnerable position, and she felt a flash of resentment at him for making her feel so defensive. And defenseless.

"I define 'back together' as exactly that," Ryan said, reaching out to run a possessive hand along the length of her bare back. Alexa shivered and clutched the sheet tighter. "That you and I are together again. And this time we're—"

"This time is all there is, Ryan." Alexa darted out of bed and snatched her plaid flannel nightshirt from the nearby chair, pulling it on quickly. She desperately needed to cover herself from his dark probing stare. "This one time. There won't be another."

"What are you saying, Alexa?" Ryan demanded, though the crushing realization began to dawn. He blocked it, refusing to consider it, to believe it.

Alexa stifled an anxious sigh. Ryan was a champion at not hearing what he didn't want to hear, at creating his own version of reality. After all, this was a man who'd invented his own world peopled with characters whose destinies he controlled completely. He undoubtedly didn't see why he couldn't exercise the same control over his own destiny. And hers, if he so chose.

Alexa swallowed hard. She was going to have to spell things out for him, and she knew it wasn't going to be pleasant. "I'm saying that we're not a couple, if that's what 'back together' means to you. We went to bed tonight and it was great, but that's all it was. Great sex. I'm not going to let you turn it into anything else."

"Great sex?" Ryan's voice echoed like thunder in the small room. He uttered an expletive.

She cast a quick, covert glance at him. He was sitting up in bed, naked and virile, and even now the sight of him impacted sensually on her. But the menacing glitter in his dark eyes immediately rallied her precarious defenses. "When you come right down to it, that's all there's ever been between us, Ryan. I realize that now, though I didn't before."

"Dammit, Alexa, you know that's not true! You loved me. You still love me. Tonight proved it!"

"Tonight proved that we're still good together in bed. Period. It doesn't mean we're going to start seeing each other again."

"The hell it doesn't!" Ryan bolted from the bed, striding forward to stand intimidatingly close to her. He towered above her, strong and determined and uncompromisingly male. "We are most definitely going to be *seeing each other.*" His inflection mocked her choice of phrase. "We're going to be seeing a lot of each other—everything there is to see."

To make his point, he ran his hand down the front of her nightshirt, possessively marking her breasts, her stomach, her thighs as his to touch.

Alexa gulped. This could get ugly. But she stood her ground. "I was honest with you, Ryan. I told you I didn't love you before we had sex, remember?"

"We made love!" Ryan corrected, incensed. "What happened between us here tonight was a hell of a lot different from a casual romp in the sack and you know it!"

"I wouldn't know," she retorted. "You're the only one I've ever romped in the sack with or made love with so it's all the same to me."

She knew instantly that she'd made a tactical error. Ryan's lips curved into a knowing, triumphant smile.

"What about this new man in your life? You haven't made love with him?" His smiled broadened. "No, you haven't," he said decisively, answering his own question. "You just said so yourself. I was your first lover and I'm also your only lover. And that bit of information unequivocally proves my point, sweetheart. You're in love with me."

He reached for her, trying to take her in his arms. Alexa ducked away. "It only proves that I'm discriminating," she said sharply, from a safer vantage point across the room. "Or maybe it proves you did such a number on me two years ago that I haven't been ready to trust a man enough to let him into my bed."

Ryan's face softened and he moved toward her again. "Honey, I know that I hurt you badly and I—"

"It doesn't matter anymore," Alexa said quickly, retreating from him. "I'm just trying to explain that—that what happened tonight doesn't prove my undying love for you. Okay, I went to bed with you. You can chalk it up to a moment of weakness. My hormones went into overdrive. You're the most sexually exciting man I've ever known and, as you so gleefully point out, you are also my only lover. Isn't there some old saying about the flesh being willing but the spirit weak?"

"You have it backward," Ryan said tightly. "The spirit is—"

"Whatever." Alexa shrugged. "You caught me at a weak moment tonight and I was carried away. After all, it *has* been a long time since..." Her explanation trailed off and she heaved a sigh. "Can we stop with the after-sex postmortems? It's getting embarrassing, Ryan."

"What are you trying to do, Alexa?" Ryan gritted. "Punish me for being stupid enough to break up with you? I don't blame you, baby, but this isn't the way. You're hurting us both by—"

"I'm not punishing you!"

"Then why are you doing this?" His voice lowered, his mouth taut. "For revenge? Is this your way of paying me back for what happened two years ago?"

"I'm not acting out of revenge!" Alexa flushed and quickly looked away.

Her blush, her obvious evasion roused his suspicions further. "Aren't you, Alexa?" he asked raspily.

"No! And stop hounding me, Ryan!"

She was uneasy mentioning revenge with Ryan because the two had been intrinsically linked when Ben went on a rampage against Ryan after the breakup, determined to retaliate for the pain he'd caused Alexa. Obviously Ryan hadn't traced to her brother the chain of mishaps that had befallen him back then. If he had, he certainly wouldn't have remained silent about it. At the very least, he might have have put it in his comic strip, for all the elements of black comedy were certainly present, including Ben as a fanatical avenging angel. At worst, Ryan could have had Ben prosecuted; he definitely had grounds to press charges.

Alexa shivered. No, the subject of revenge was one to avoid around Ryan Cassidy. In fact, she shouldn't discuss anything with Ryan Cassidy, unless it involved his daughter's condition. She'd made a major mistake tonight, crossing the protective line from professional to intimate, and there was nothing else to do but admit it and move on. Beginning right now.

"I was wrong to let you come in, wrong to talk to you, and absolutely crazy to make love with you tonight, Ryan."

"No, you weren't, baby. You love me and you acted on it. There's nothing wrong with that. But what you're doing now..." He shook his head, running his hand frustratedly through the thickness of his hair. "The denial, the game-playing. That's wrong, Alexa. And totally unlike you."

"And this long-suffering understanding and analytical skills are totally unlike you," Alexa shot back. "Well, maybe we've both changed, hmm, Ryan? It seems we've switched roles. This time *you* can be the sincere one with

stars in your eyes who truly believes in happy endings. *I* get
to be the manipulative, deceitful snake.''

"You can't have changed that much, Alexa." His jaw
tightened. "And I know you would never sleep with one
man for kicks while you're supposedly involved with another."

Of course she wouldn't, Alexa silently agreed. Unfortunately, according to the scenario she'd presented, she'd done
exactly that tonight. She frowned. This was getting way too
complicated; she was confused and dispirited. Exhaustion,
both emotional and physical, came crashing down on her
and she suddenly felt weak and teary.

"I want you to leave, Ryan," she ordered, and wished
that her tone sounded more commanding. She tried a little
harder. "Get dressed and get out."

She was relieved and a little surprised when Ryan actually ceded to her wishes, picking up his clothes and pulling
them on, his expression grim. She left the room to keep
from watching him.

He joined her in her small living room a few moments
later, fully dressed. Something feminine and primitive rip-
pled through her at the sight of her lover. The mere thought
of him in that role, combined with the memory of their
tempestuous mating, brought a flood of hot color to her
cheeks.

"Before I go, I'd like to ask you something," he said,
gazing at her steadily.

Alexa could feel the tense energy coiled within him and
silently admonished herself for being so attuned to him. It
seemed to be an ongoing talent she possessed, this innate
sensitivity to his moods. Too bad she was totally in the dark
as to his thoughts and motives. Those she could only speculate upon, and she'd managed to err every time.

"You can ask but I may not answer," she said, shifting
uneasily under his mesmerizing dark gaze. "Or you may not
like my answer." She was already certain she wasn't going
to like the question.

"Does this boyfriend of yours even exist?" Ryan demanded bluntly.

Alexa suppressed a groan. "Of—of course he exists," she stammered. Why did Ryan have to resurrect that issue now? But the deception did offer some protection against Ryan's infuriating insistence that she still loved him. Her pride demanded a defense after her ardent surrender to him tonight.

"Yet you're unable to come up with this guy's name?" Ryan wasn't even making a pretense of believing her.

Alexa stared at his strong-boned face, handsome but hard and sardonic too. He was well versed in games people played, because he was a skilled game-player himself. Now he'd caught her in an age-old one: inventing a rival to inspire jealousy or salvage pride. Well, she was doing neither, Alexa decided. She was being governed by sheer self-preservation.

"Not unable, just unwilling," she snapped. "Why should I tell you anything?"

Ryan merely smiled a maddeningly smug smile. "Why, indeed? You've already told me everything I need to know." He leaned down and kissed the top of her head. "You need a little time and space tonight and I'm willing to give it to you. Good night, baby. I'll see you in the morning." He strode jauntily to the door, grinning.

That satisfied smirk, his self-confidence that bordered intolerably on arrogance. Alexa's temper flared, ignited like a match striking flint. He really thought he had her now! Take her to bed and the past two years are negated. A simple "I want you back" and she was supposed to forget all about the pain and betrayal and loss of trust.

Well, she hadn't forgotten a single thing. "His name is Nathaniel!" Her voice, taut with anger and challenge, halted him in his tracks. "Nathaniel Tremaine."

She didn't have a plethora of bachelors to choose from, and Nathaniel's was the first name to spring to mind. They'd been thrown together a number of times due to their respective ties to Carrie and Tyler, and Nathaniel had made his usual, almost obligatory pass at Alexa that he made at every woman he encountered. She had been somewhat amused by him but not even remotely tempted.

"Nathaniel Tremaine," Ryan repeated. He turned to face her, his hand still on the doorknob. "You're not serious."

"I'm dating Nathaniel Tremaine," she reiterated, a little more strongly now. "He's Tyler's brother and he's an executive with Tremaine Incorporated. Nathaniel is—"

"An idiot," Ryan interjected. "I happen to know Nathaniel Tremaine and he is no more your type than—"

"You are?" Alexa suggested acidly.

"Nathaniel Tremaine is a vacuous goof-off who still behaves like an overaged fraternity boy and who simply coasts along in that nothing job his family created for him in their company. Talking to him is like carrying on a conversation with an air-headed adolescent. He's a spoiled playboy who can't hold two thoughts in his head at the same time. And you are not dating him, Alexa."

"Yes, I am," Alexa said, delighted by his ire. She'd hit the jackpot with this one. "It sounds like you don't like Nathaniel very much, Ryan."

"Liking him has nothing to do with it. I don't respect him, nobody does. His own family considers him an exasperating nitwit. And no wonder, he is one. He's the perfect match for Storm or Sky, both of whom he has dated and who might even be his intellectual superiors. A daunting notion, to be sure."

"Well." Alexa folded her arms, wondering how to counter that impassioned diatribe. Unfortunately everything Ryan had said was true; she hadn't expected him to be so knowledgeable on the subject of Nathaniel Tremaine. Too bad he'd dated the ex-stepsisters. "You have your opinion of Nathaniel and I have mine. I happen to enjoy his company and our—our relationship is progressing nicely. Not that it's any business of yours!"

"Call him," Ryan said.

She stared at him. "What?"

"Give Nathaniel a call right now." Ryan's eyes gleamed with challenge. "That shouldn't pose a problem for you, if you two are involved in such a *nice relationship,* hmm?"

"You don't believe me? You think I'm making it up?" Alexa was outraged.

"No, I don't believe you," Ryan replied, his voice and smile taunting. "And yes, I think you're making it up. So call him and prove me wrong—if you can."

"I certainly can! And—and I will. But I—I have to look up his number first."

"Haven't memorized it?" Ryan mocked.

"I haven't had to. Nathaniel calls me regularly."

Her stomach lurching, Alexa stalked into her bedroom and thumbed through the phone directory. Ryan stood on the threshold, watching with a sardonic smile. She hoped against hope for an unlisted number, but alas, there it was— Nathaniel Tremaine's name, address and telephone number.

Why on earth was she doing this? Alexa wondered grimly, as she punched the numbers on her touch-tone phone. She didn't have to prove anything to Ryan Cassidy; she ought to kick him out of her apartment with no explanations and no apologies. The fact that she'd been caught up in this game of one-upmanship—had even instigated this particular round!—was appalling and unnerving. She didn't want to speculate on what it meant. She refused to even hazard a guess.

But she stayed on the line as it rang and rang. When an answering machine finally clicked on, Alexa breathed a heartfelt sigh of relief. Her eyes holding Ryan's, she left a message. "Hi, Nathaniel. Just wanted to give you a quick call to—" She paused.

Ryan had just rolled his eyes heavenward. Alexa scowled back at him. "To tell you that I'd love to see you tomorrow. How about dinner, my treat? Give me a call and let me know. Bye...honey."

She replaced the receiver in its cradle, aware that her hand was shaking and that her heart was pounding as if she'd just run laps. "I did it," she exclaimed, flashing a victorious smile at Ryan.

"You didn't leave your name and number," Ryan pointed out laconically.

"I didn't have to. He'll know it's me." Alexa kept a straight face, but she was laughing inwardly. Not only had she bested Ryan Cassidy, but Nathaniel Tremaine would be confounded by the anonymous message on the tape. Not a bad finish for what had started as a intolerably dull and dreary evening.

She glanced at the clock on her nightstand. "It's getting late, Ryan," she said pointedly.

"And you're tired."

"Yes."

"Did I wear you out tonight, sweetheart?" His voice was mocking but held a caressive note.

Alexa frowned. She might have scored a point with the Nathaniel Tremaine phone call but Ryan was still regarding her with a possessive arrogance that made her hackles rise. "It won't happen again," she said resolutely. "Tonight was a—a one-night stand, Ryan. One that won't be repeated."

"So you've said." His dark gaze swept over the bed, rumpled from their vigorous bout of passion. "Want me to tuck you in?"

Her eyes narrowed to slits. She wouldn't dignify that with a response. "Goodnight, Ryan."

He was watching her intently, his expression thoughtful and assessing. "Goodnight, Alexa," he said at last. Still he made no movement to leave. "Walk me to the door?" he suggested huskily.

"You know the way out. It's certainly not hard to find the door in a three-room apartment."

"True. But you have to deadbolt the lock and put the chain on after I go."

Alexa sighed impatiently. "You sound like my father. He's a safety nut, too."

"Believe me, my feelings for you are as far from paternal as you can get. How is your dad, anyway?"

Ryan tried to put his arm around her as they walked to the front door together. Alexa deliberately moved away, out of his reach. "Dad and Mom are in Germany right now. He's a colonel in the Air Force."

"I haven't forgotten who your father is and what he does," Ryan reminded her quietly. "I remember everything you told me, Alexa. About you and about—"

"I remember everything you said back then too, Ryan," she cut in. "And everything you didn't say as well. Which is why this reconciliation whim of yours is doomed to fail. "

"It's not a whim, Alexa. And it's going to happen." At the door, he suddenly wrapped his arms around her and pulled her tightly against him.

Eight

Alexa gasped in surprise and was about to pull away when Ryan's mouth descended on hers for a hard possessive kiss. She gave up all thoughts of jerking herself out of his arms as hot passion instantly boiled up between them once again.

She ran her arms around Ryan's neck, caressing his broad shoulders and sighing against his mouth in sweet surrender. The kiss went on and on, and when he finally lifted his lips from hers, both were dazed and breathless.

"I told myself that I wouldn't ask again, that you would have to be the one to do the asking," Ryan said raggedly. "But all my brave intentions are shot to hell...I'm not only asking, I'm willing to beg...Alexa, please let me stay with you tonight."

She wanted to say yes so much, it alarmed her. *Why couldn't he spend the night, just this once?* The insidious rationalizations were starting all over again and seemed just as reasonable this time as they had earlier. A line of thought that led inexorably to the bedroom.

Just this once.

"No!" Alexa exclaimed a little frantically, dragging herself out of his arms. Resuming her physical relationship with Ryan Cassidy would lead to disaster—for her. She knew that now with a certainty that was suddenly, blindingly clear.

"I can't. I—I don't love you, Ryan," she insisted. It was suddenly extremely important that she keep reminding herself of that fact. She would *not* give in to passion with a man she didn't love, not again. 'Just this once' meant exactly that. Once.

"Love is based on trust and I don't trust you. How can I, Ryan? You threw my love back in my face and coolly walked away, and you stayed away for two years. You would've been perfectly content to spend the rest of your life without me if Kelsey's accident hadn't thrown us together again."

"I haven't been perfectly content. I've been disconnected and lonely, with no joy or purpose. I couldn't have spent the rest of my life that way. Sweetheart, I know I would've come back to you even if Kelsey hadn't been hurt. It might've taken me a little bit longer to realize what—"

"It's a nice fairy tale and you might've even talked yourself into believing it, but I don't, Ryan." Her voice brooked no argument. Alexa the naive dreamer had evolved into Alexa the realist.

"You have to, Alexa, it's true. I—I love you!"

His impassioned declaration astonished them both.

"That's the first time you've ever said that to me." Alexa remembered how much she'd yearned to hear those words from him, how often she'd dreamed of them. Back in the old days when she'd loved him. It was a lamentable quirk of fate that he'd said them now, when it didn't matter anymore. Oddly, she felt like crying.

Ryan shrugged uncomfortably. Some words were difficult, even for a clever wordsmith such as he. "I—assumed you knew. There are some things that go without saying," he mumbled.

His unease irritated her, and her mood veered wildly from sadness to anger. "You went without saying it, all right," she snapped. "Even in bed. Why, even tonight you didn't—"

"Well, I'm saying it now," he cut in sharply. "I love you, Alexa."

"No, you don't."

"First you complain that I haven't said it, now you contradict me?"

"I don't believe you love me. I can't believe it."

"Then I'll have to convince you, won't I?" But how? Ryan fought a sickening sense of loss. When he'd come here tonight, he had fully expected to patch things up with Alexa, to make love to her. Well, he'd succeeded in taking her to bed but not in winning her back.

"I'm not giving up," Ryan insisted fiercely. "You might say you don't love me but you do want me, Alexa. Tonight proved that."

Alexa winced. It was pointless to deny the desire he aroused in her, not after she'd succumbed so completely to it. But she wasn't going to be tricked into confusing sex with love again, no matter how tempting and potent the passion. "I don't have to give in to it. I won't. It's not right for me, Ryan."

They stared at each other for a long moment. "I could show you how right it is. I could take you in my arms and it wouldn't be long before I'd be carrying you back to bed, with you wanting it as much as I do," he grated.

Alexa made no reply. They both knew what he said was true.

"But the lady said no." Ryan heaved a heavy sigh. "Hard as it is to accept, I guess I have to."

He was out the door before Alexa could even blink with surprise. She stared after him, into the empty hallway for a few dazed minutes before she quietly closed the door and locked it.

Ryan had actually ceded to her wishes when they ran counter to his own? Especially when they both knew how quickly and how easily he could have arranged a different outcome, the one he favored. Alexa was astonished. His actions didn't compute with what she knew of Ryan Cassidy, the man who demanded his own way in everything from storyline approval to sex.

She didn't know what to make of it, she didn't know what to think of him. How could she make the pieces fit when she didn't have a clear picture of what was going on with either of them? The urge to talk things out with her sister was overwhelming, and when the phone rang a half hour later, she wasn't too surprised to hear Carrie's voice on the other end of the line. The bond between the sisters was deep; this wasn't the first time one's concentrated thoughts seemed to conjure the other up.

"Alexa, is it true?" Carrie demanded incredulously.

"W-what?" Alexa was stunned. Though they were emotionally in tune, they'd never shared an episode of mind reading. Her heart pounded. How was she going to explain to her sister about Ryan Cassidy and what had happened tonight, when she couldn't even explain it to herself?

But it seemed she wouldn't have to. "Nathaniel called Tyler a few minutes ago, gloating over a message he claims you left on his answering machine," Carrie exclaimed. "Something about you offering to take him to dinner tomorrow. He was bragging that he'd *bagged* you at last. Those were his exact words." Carrie made an exclamation of disgust. "Alexa, I know Ben thinks it would be advantageous for you to hook up with Nathaniel but—oh, Alexa, say it isn't so. Nathaniel is—"

"I know, I know. A goof-off, a playboy. Have no fears, Carrie, I'm not harboring a secret passion for your brother-in-law."

"And the message on his machine? He claims to have a 'photostatic memory' for voices, if there is such a thing. He swears it was you, even though you didn't leave your name."

"The guy is delusional as well as egocentric. If he calls me, I'll tell him so."

Carrie laughed. "I told Tyler that Nathaniel was indulging in some powerful wishful thinking! You with Nathaniel Tremaine—ha! That's about as likely as you taking up with Ryan Cassidy again!"

"That is highly unlikely," Alexa agreed, holding on to the thought. Talking to Carrie had helped. She already felt stronger, filled with resolve. "In fact, it's impossible," she added more forcefully.

"You'll agree to a date with Nathaniel Tremaine on the same day you tell Ryan Cassidy you want him back," joked Carrie. "That will be the same day that I meet Elvis in a bowling alley and Ben finds his long-lost evil twin . . . which would make us quadruplets, I guess."

"Ben *is* the evil twin, it's the virtuous brother who's long-lost," Alexa pointed out. "But I get your point, Carrie."

A relationship with Ryan Cassidy, however renewed and improved, was an absurdity too foolish to consider. And a risk too dangerous for her heart to take.

"I sure do wish you good luck today, honey," Gloria greeted Alexa at the front door the next morning. The older woman looked exasperated and disapproving.

Alexa tensed. From the moment she'd awakened from a fitful sleep at dawn, she'd been nervous about seeing Ryan again. Wondering if he would continue to proclaim his newfound devotion to her. Wondering if he would ignore her. Rehearsing what she would do and say in both instances. One thing she hadn't considered was Ryan telling anyone about last night's interlude. If Gloria knew . . .

"Why are you wishing me luck? Am I going to need it?" Even to herself, she sounded overly apprehensive.

"Oh yes, indeed." Gloria smiled grimly. "They're all on the warpath today. Melissa arrived in the middle of breakfast because she's working the early shift at the restaurant.

She brought her little boy with her, and Ryan was in a rotten mood because his car was vandalized last night and—"

"Vandalized?" Alexa interrupted. She thought of his black 1963 Corvette Stingray parked in the lot next to her apartment building last night. "Which car was it?"

"The black one, I think. I hardly know one from the other." Gloria shook her head. "They might be collectibles to him but they're just old cars to me. He took the car out last night and parked it where some hoodlums marked it all up. Looks like they took coins and scratched drawings and nasty words all over it."

"Is it ruined?" Alexa held her breath.

"Well, it does look bad. The body certainly needs to be refinished and repainted. But it's fixable, I think. I told Ryan not to be so disturbed. A couple years ago someone poured a pound of sugar into the gas tank of one of his other old cars and it totally destroyed the engine. Now that's what I call ruined! Last night wasn't nearly as bad as that."

Alexa remembered Ben's triumphant expression two years ago, when he'd told her and Carrie about what he had done to a certain car with a certain bag of sugar. About how revenge on Ryan Cassidy had to take a material tack since emotional retribution would be useless on a stone-hearted monster such as he. Alexa had been horrified by Ben's actions, then terrified he would be caught.

Discreet inquiries to an attorney friend yielded the information that Ben's actions would constitute charges of criminal mischief and destruction of private property—not to mention a civil suit to collect damages. Knowing Ryan's attachment to his beloved cars, both were a distinct possibility. Alexa and Carrie had worried for months about Ben's fate should Ryan learn the truth. Ben, however, was cavalier and unrepentant. So much so that for one awful moment, Alexa wondered if her brother had been lurking in her neighborhood last night with a coin.

No, she decided. If he had defaced Ryan's car, she'd have heard about it by now. Ben was not one to keep his vengeful deeds to himself. He would have called her and Carrie, to boast of his latest triumph. She recalled how he couldn't wait to tell how he'd unleashed those six pigeons in Ryan's condo two years ago, where the birds spent an entire weekend alone, cooped up inside.

Gloria picked up her narrative. "Anyway, Melissa's boy threw a tantrum about something and wouldn't stop shrieking. Ryan made some remark about needing earplugs, and of course Melissa lit into him. She is so defensive! Poor Ryan can't say anything right as far as she's concerned. I know he might have sounded a bit testy, but he was really just kidding about the child screaming loud enough to summon every volunteer firefighting company in the county."

"Breakfast with the Cassidys," Alexa murmured. "A delight."

"Then into the middle of the fray comes the newest tutor, sent over by the school." Gloria sighed. "Kelsey took an instant dislike to the poor man and instructed her little brother to throw a jar of jelly at him. Who would have dreamed that a two-year-old child would have such dead aim? The jar hit the tutor smack in the stomach and jelly spilled all over him. It was the running kind, of course. The poor man was a mess! Melissa and Ryan both scolded Kelsey, and then that wretched little girl just grabbed the end of the tablecloth and yanked it off the table. Dishes, food, juice, hot coffee—everything went flying. Everybody got hit with something."

"And the tutor fled for his life?" Alexa surmised.

"Who wouldn't?" Gloria scowled. "It looked like a crazy house. I told them so, and of course that simply started another round of the blame game."

"Where is everybody now?"

"Melissa and Kyle left, Ryan is holed up in his studio and Kelsey is sulking in her room. I felt I should warn you. It's still pretty tense around here. Are you sure you want to stay?"

"I'll stay," Alexa said firmly. "I'm not going to be driven off like those hapless tutors."

"Good!" Gloria beamed her approval. "This household can use someone like you. Someone levelheaded, someone even-tempered, someone not driven by their emotions."

"I'd hardly call Ryan emotional," Alexa said. At Gloria's quizzical glance she added quickly, "I mean, he's so cool and flippant." That was the way she'd always thought of him, until his impassioned entreaties of last night. Her cheeks burned. Last night he had been ardent and intense, not flip or cool at all.

"That's the image he chooses to present," Gloria said, sighing. "But if you knew Ryan well, you'd know it just a front. He cares deeply about who and what matters to him. And he doesn't give a damn about what doesn't interest him and won't pretend to. Oh, Ryan might seem cold but he's not. How could he be, with his Irish and his Spanish blood? Two passionate races there, hmm?"

Alexa nodded, a little uncertainly.

"Our great-grandfather emigrated from Spain, and the family ultimately wound up in Miami," Gloria continued proudly. "That's where Isabella met Ronald Cassidy. They were devoted to each other and a happy family with young Ryan. Isabella's death was tragic. Ron seemed to lose his bearings afterward. It was heartbreaking to see him turn into a completely different person from the man we had known and loved. The chain of unsuitable women he married, the way he alternately neglected and was cruel to his son . . . it was a steady deterioration, terrible to observe."

Gloria shuddered. "Poor Ryan floundered. I watched him turn from a warm sensitive child into a guarded, cynical young man. And Melissa . . ." She threw up her hands. "What can I say? She was all wrong for Ryan. Her mother is of Serbian descent, her father Croatian. She's a civil war unto herself."

"I suppose that makes Kelsey an international basket case if you believe nationality affects personality." Alexa shrugged. "I don't believe it myself."

"Speaks the all-American girl." Gloria laughed indulgently. "I guess you don't need to be wished good luck. You make your own, eh?"

"Let's just say I don't hold my ethnic origins accountable for my actions," Alexa said lightly. Although it would certainly be more comfortable to pin the blame for last night's interlude with Ryan on a set of volatile great-grandparents instead of her own loss of control.

She set off for Kelsey's bedroom. A Barbie doll came whizzing past her head the moment she stepped inside the room. Alexa strategically ducked and the doll hit the wall and fell to the floor.

Alexa picked it up. "From what I've heard, Kyle wouldn't have missed his target. He's an ace marksman, especially when it comes to flinging jelly at tutors."

Kelsey glowered at her. "Give me my doll!" she demanded.

"So you can throw it at me again? Not a chance, Kelsey."

"I have lots more I can throw," Kelsey warned, leaning over the side of the bed to reach into a big box of dolls and doll clothes. Her movements were halting and awkward. Within moments, she'd lost her balance and fallen out of bed onto the floor.

The girl began to scream at the top of her lungs, from temper and frustration not pain, Alexa was certain of that. The carpet was too thick and the height of the bed too low for any injury to be sustained from her fall. Except to her pride.

Kelsey was enraged. "I hate you!" she shrieked at Alexa. "Go away, get out of my house." She repeated the litany over and over.

Her screams brought Gloria and Ryan running. Gloria took one look at the scene, crossed herself and left the room. Ryan picked up the thrashing, furious child from the floor and put her back on the bed, all the while fending off her flailing fists.

"I hate you, Daddy!" Kelsey yelled. "I hate you and Mommy and Gloria and Alexa and Dr. Ellender and that stupid teacher and—"

"Kelsey, calm down," Ryan said with surprising sternness.

Kelsey halted, mid-tirade, to glare at him. "I can do whatever I want. I don't have to listen to you. I hate you and Mom—"

"Is there anyone you don't hate, Kelsey?" Alexa asked, her bland tone sharply contrasting with the others' sharp anger. She focused all her attention on the child, ignoring Ryan.

She had to. Her heart had jumped alarmingly at the sight of him. His face was shadowed and unshaved and so compellingly virile, she felt her pulses hammering in every part of her body. Images of them kissing, caressing, their bodies surging together, were superimposed in her mind, momentarily taking her out of the present and catapulting her back into the passionate heat of last night.

Kelsey stopped howling to stare disdainfully at Alexa.

The abrupt silence blanketing the room, so at odds with the raucous noise a moment ago, jarred Alexa out of her erotic reverie. Flushed and shaken, she kept her eyes fixed on the little girl but she was achingly, unnervingly aware of Ryan. When he turned his head, when he made even the slightest movement, she knew it.

"I don't hate my little brother," Kelsey announced, after some thought.

"Well, you won't be much use to your little brother if you're stuck permanently in bed," Alexa said matter-of-factly.

She heard Ryan inhale sharply and cast a quick glance at him. Both pain and anger were reflected in his eyes but he said nothing. She forced herself to concentrate solely on

Kelsey and it wasn't easy. Her gaze, her thoughts, were drawn to Ryan like filings to a magnet.

Kelsey's dark brown eyes darted from Ryan to Alexa. When her daddy didn't leap to her defense, she glared banefully at her therapist. "I'm not going to be stuck in bed," she snarled. "I'm gonna get better and then I'll take Kyle and run away. Nobody will ever find us again and then they'll be sorry!"

"A revenge fantasy can be a powerful motivator," Alexa remarked. "Do you know what that means?"

"No!" Kelsey snapped.

"It means if you really want to get out of that bed and back on your feet, you'll do your exercises. Starting now." Alexa turned to Ryan but she didn't meet his eyes. She kept her gaze focused on the bright orange wall behind him. "If you'll excuse us, Ryan, we have work to do."

It was humbling to admit that she wouldn't be able to work effectively with him there, but for the sake of her patient, Alexa faced the truth. Like it or not—and she didn't!—Ryan Cassidy was a major distraction.

"I'm gonna get better enough to run away," Kelsey spit out, a malicious smile on her small face. "And you can't stop me—Ryan," she added, throwing her ultimate insult at him.

Ryan opened his mouth to speak, then abruptly closed it again and strode from the room.

"Ryan, hmm?" Alexa stared thoughtfully at her young patient. "You really are mad at your dad today, aren't you?" She began to massage her left foot.

"He yelled at me at breakfast. I want Jack to be my dad," Kelsey announced.

"Jack never yells at you?"

If looks could kill, Alexa would have been vaporized by the hostile glare Kelsey directed at her. "He didn't yell at me *today*," she muttered crossly.

"I understand. So you're Kelsey Webber today." Alexa continued her ministrations. "Did I get the name right?"

"That's right. Ouch!" Kelsey let out a bloodcurdling yell. "That hurts!"

"Your muscle is contracting," Alexa explained and continued to capably massage the foot. Kelsey cried out again.

"I know it hurts, Kelsey, but it's a good sign." Alexa's pale blue eyes glowed with excitement. "A very good sign. It means the swelling has gone down and reduced the pressure around the vertebrae that affects those muscles. Do you understand what that means, Kelsey?"

"No," Kelsey's voice rose excitedly. Alexa's enthusiasm was catching. "But it's something good, right?"

"Very, very good. Can you feel this, Kelsey?" She pinched her big toe.

Kelsey's eyes widened. "I can feel it! It doesn't hurt but I felt it."

"It feels more like pressure than a pinch," Alexa explained. "Now close your eyes and tell me if you can feel where I'm pinching."

Kelsey's lids snapped shut and Alexa pinched the sole of her foot, the skin on her foot and ankle, her calf and her knee. Kelsey shrieked "yes" each time and correctly identified each place she'd been pinched. They tried it on her other leg with similar results.

"Kelsey, this is wonderful. It means you're getting sensation back and that's a very good indication you'll regain full movement." Alexa grabbed her in a heartfelt bear hug. "We'll have to work extra hard but it'll be worth it, honey."

Kelsey hugged her back. "I couldn't feel anything but now I can. Pretty soon I'll be able to move my legs again and then I'll be walking." Her chocolate-brown eyes misted with tears. "I hate being paralyzed, Alexa."

Alexa's eyes filled too. "I know, Kelsey."

"I get into real bad moods sometimes 'cause I can't do the things I used to."

"It must make you furious. And sad, too." Alexa resumed the muscle-stretching regime.

Kelsey nodded. "Sometimes my mom and dad make me furious, too. Sometimes I really do want to run away."

"Do you ever wish they'd get back together?" Alexa asked curiously, now working on the other leg. "I've heard that many children of divorced parents want their mother and father to remarry and live together as a family again."

"I don't remember living with both my parents. I was just a baby when they got divorced." Kelsey looked thoughtful. "They don't like each other very much. I can't even picture them living in the same house. I don't want them to get married to each other, but I wish they wouldn't fight so much."

Alexa nodded sympathetically.

"I wish Mommy would marry Jack," Kelsey said.

"And what about your father?" Alexa pressed. She felt a guilty blush of shame stain her cheeks. True, it was useful and distracting to make conversation with her patients while working with them, but pumping Kelsey about Ryan was out of line and she knew it. So why didn't she shut up and change the subject? Instead she heard herself ask, "Do you want him to get married?"

"To who?" Kelsey asked.

She'd deserved that, Alexa admonished herself. Her face and neck flushed scarlet. "No one in particular. Never mind, let's get you into the workout room so you can use the equipment. We have a lot to do, Kelsey."

"I never met any of Daddy's girlfriends." Kelsey wasn't quite ready to let the subject drop. "I don't think he has one. But Mommy says—"

"Let's see you get yourself into the wheelchair," Alexa interrupted heartily. She didn't want to hear what Mommy had said. She didn't want to talk anymore about Ryan Cassidy. She put him firmly from her mind for the rest of the morning while she worked with his daughter.

Shortly after noon, Alexa turned Kelsey over to Gloria, declined their invitation to join them for lunch and headed swiftly out of the house, toward her car. She wasn't running from another encounter with Ryan, she assured herself. She certainly wasn't hiding from him. But when he seemed to materialize out of nowhere to join her, her insides churned and her heart thundered against her ribs as if she actually had been surreptitiously running and hiding—and had just been caught.

The sun shone brilliantly through the red, orange and gold leaves of the trees, casting a warm glow on Ryan's jeans and denim jacket. Alexa drew the lapels of her own thick blue sweater coat around her, more a protective gesture against Ryan's nearness than from the cold, although a stiff breeze was blowing.

"Kelsey made progress this morning," she said quickly, before he could speak. "I'll give you a detailed report at the end of the week, but I can tell you now that things look very promising."

The wind whipped a strand of her hair across her face. Ryan took it between his fingers and gently tucked it behind her left ear. Alexa trembled.

"I just wanted to thank you," he said huskily. "For sticking with Kelsey after the brouhaha this morning."

"All in a day's work," she said lightly. "I've been in worse brouhahas."

"And do you often have to work with bad-tempered spoiled brats like Kelsey?"

Alexa's eyes widened. The other day he'd excoriated her for referring to Kelsey as spoiled. Now he was saying the same, and a lot worse, about his beloved daughter.

"Kelsey is bright and determined and can be very sweet," she said diplomatically, feeling a need to defend her young patient. But a dose of realism was definitely required as well. "However, she does have some problems that aren't due solely to the accident and her injuries."

"I know. I'm finally beginning to realize that." Ryan heaved a dispirited sigh. "Some part of me recognized a long time ago how angry and manipulative Kelsey is, but I refused to admit it because it would also mean admitting that I'd made some major mistakes as her father. Having experienced Ron Cassidy for a father, I wanted to be the perfect dad. I wanted my kid to feel loved and wanted and to know that her father would always be there for her."

"I think Kelsey does know that," Alexa said softly. "But you and Melissa have got to come to a truce, for Kelsey's sake. You've given her way too much power for a little girl. She doesn't want to see her parents at each other's throats, but she'll keep pitting you against each other as long as you allow her to do it."

"That's easier said than done. Melissa uses her to—"

Alexa silenced him with a glance that spoke volumes.

Ryan grimaced sheepishly. "I guess it's a whole lot easier to lay the blame for everything on Melissa."

"Melissa loves Kelsey, Ryan. And Kelsey loves her."

"It just that Melissa isn't my idea of a real mother," protested Ryan. "She's nothing like my mother who was patient and gentle and soft-spoken. Melissa is angry and shrill, quarrelsome and overly dramatic and—"

"Melissa has her own less-than-flattering description of you, too," Alexa cut in. "Both of you are so steeped in negatives, you don't have a single positive word to say about each other. You each see the other as completely one-dimensional, and that one dimension is all bad. It doesn't jibe with reality, Ryan. Will you, at the very least, admit that perhaps Melissa isn't at her best around you? That there may be a side of her, a good and loving side, that you've seldom seen?"

"Make that have *never* seen," Ryan grumbled. "But, yes, I see your point. If only Melissa could. Would you ever consider giving this lecture to her?"

"Yes, I'll talk to her, if you'll give me an assurance that you don't intend to seek custody of Kelsey. If Melissa weren't so threatened and terrified of losing Kelsey, chances are she would be less hostile and more reasonable."

Ryan stared silently into space for a long time, a range of expressions crossing his face, from frowning denial to pensive, and finally to humorous. "Well, Melissa was angry with Kelsey when she told little Kyle to throw the jelly at the teacher this morning," he said at last. "That was unexpected. I expected her to cheer the kids on because I'd reprimanded Kelsey but she didn't."

"So you see, you can agree on something—that children shouldn't pelt teachers with jelly, particularly not the runny kind." Alexa smiled. "A small thing maybe, but it is a step toward some common ground, Ryan."

She took a deep breath. Ryan was watching her, his dark eyes brooding and intense. He was standing between her and her car door, blocking her escape. She cleared her throat, more than a little nervous. Of his nearness, of her own tempestuous reaction to it. And most of all, of the aura of intimacy that seemed to enclose and engulf them.

"Okay, I'll drop it." His voice was deep and low and decisive. "You can tell Melissa that I won't sue for custody of Kelsey."

Alexa stared at him, blinking in disbelief. She'd sent up the custody issue as a trial balloon, never expecting him to agree but floating the idea for some future consideration. It was astonishing, it was exhilarating, for him to have listened to her and then made a decision based on her advice.

It was a heady sensation that made her feel as effective and exultant as she did when her young patients made an important breakthrough, thanks to her skill and their resolve. A winning combination of two people working together to improve and achieve success. She did it every day in her professional life but she'd never dreamed of sharing such an affinity with Ryan. Only in the bedroom had they ever approached the rapport and mutuality she felt with him and for him, right now.

She could hardly believe it. Ryan had shared his deepest concerns about his child, he'd bared his soul to her, admitting that he was wrong, an impossibility for his arrogant I-know-what's-best-for-everyone former alter ego. Today they'd talked, *really talked,* listening and actually hearing each other.

Their conversation this morning, though brief, was deeper and more significant than any and all they'd had during the entire eight months of their previous relationship. Back then, they had bantered, they'd teased and taunted and fought. But they had never really reached each other. Alexa realized that now.

And suddenly, it was too much, it was too intense. She felt panicky and uncertain. The Ryan Cassidy who had betrayed her, the man she didn't love because she didn't dare trust him again, seemed a safer and more familiar figure than this man who stood before her.

"I think you should be the one to tell Melissa about dropping the custody suit," she said, fixing her gaze on a squirrel who was running across a nearby tree limb. Alexa could feel Ryan's eyes on her, knew he was willing her to look at him.

She resisted. She had to regain her emotional equilibrium and knew she would lose it completely if drawn into his deep, dark gaze. "Melissa won't believe it unless it comes from you," she added.

"She probably won't believe it then, either," Ryan said wryly. "She'll accuse me of some kind of trickery or deceit, of trying to lure her into a false sense of security before I launch my sneak attack."

"Not if you approach her seriously, as a concerned father to a concerned mother, minus your smirk and that insolent, always-so-cool attitude of yours."

Ryan arched his brows, grinning wickedly. "You know me so well." He suddenly exuded that insolent, always-so-cool attitude. The instant transformation was startling.

"No." Alexa shook her head. "I don't know you at all, Ryan." Her head was spinning. Would the real Ryan Cassidy please stand up? Was there a real Ryan Cassidy or was he simply playing various roles, detached from each one, unknown and unknowable to those who dared to love him?

Not that she was one of those, Alexa hastened to assure herself. Her days of loving Ryan Cassidy were definitely over. She felt a fierce compelling urge to run away from him. To get away right now, before she either kicked him or kissed him, for she feared she was on the verge of doing either, or both. He provoked such wildness in her. Involuntarily she flashed back to last night's passionate idyll. A dangerous wildness.

Alexa glanced at her watch, her defenses fully activated. "I really have to go, I'm running late," she blurted out. "I work at the Children's Rehabilitation Institute this afternoon and I have a full patient load scheduled."

"You don't have to run away from me, Alexa. You don't have to be afraid of me, either."

Alexa, already seated behind the wheel of her car, glanced up at him. "I'm not running away," she insisted, perhaps a bit too emphatically. "And I'm certainly not afraid of you."

"Prove it," he challenged. "Have dinner with me tonight."

She felt oddly light-headed. A date with Ryan? A premeditated decision to go out with him seemed an even greater surrender than her spontaneous, physical one last night. It was a walk on the wild side that Alexa knew she wasn't ready to take.

"Sorry, I have other plans," she said with what she hoped passed for breezy insouciance.

"Do these alleged plans involve your alleged boyfriend Nathaniel Tremaine?"

That superior smirk and insolent, always-so-cool attitude of his were firmly in place. There wasn't a trace of the contemplative, caring man she'd bonded with only a few moments ago. Alexa frowned.

"What my plans do not involve is *you,*" she said succinctly.

She rolled up the window, gunned the engine and took off before Ryan had a chance to reply. Or a chance to try to change her mind.

Not that he could have, she assured herself as she sped along the beltway. Or could he?

She slowed as a police cruiser appeared ahead. The point wasn't lost on her. Just as she'd needed the sight of those flashing red and blue lights to remind her to slow down, she also seemed to need a tangible reminder to keep her reckless impulses in check when it came to Ryan. If only she could find one.

Nine

"Tyler, look at this beauty! A snow-white 1965 Ford Mustang!" Ben's exultant voice sounded above the noise of the crowd viewing the cars at the American classic-car show.

"Tyler already owns a '65 Mustang, Ben," said Carrie Shaw Tremaine. Her hand was tucked into her husband's, and they smiled at each other, amused by Ben's ingratiating enthusiasm for classic sports cars.

"But not a snow-white one!" Ben exclaimed. "Oh man, do you see that Pontiac GTO over there? It's incredible, Tyler!"

"I didn't know your brother was such an old sports-car nut," Nathaniel Tremaine remarked to Alexa.

"He's not," Alexa said bluntly. "But since Tyler is, Ben is willing to play the part of one. If Tyler displayed an interest in big game animals, Ben would organize a safari. If Tyler was into archaeology, Ben would raid an ancient burial site for artifacts."

Nathaniel looked puzzled. "I don't get it."

Alexa sighed and cast a weary glance at her unofficial escort of the evening. Vacuous, Ryan had called him. That didn't even come close.

"Ben wants to be Tyler's best friend," she explained patiently. She didn't add why. After all, Nathaniel couldn't hold two thoughts in his head at the same time. She smiled, recalling Ryan's nasty but all-too-accurate barb.

Nathaniel thought her smile was meant for him and immediately acted on it. He tried to take her hand but Alexa slipped them both into the pockets of her jacket. He tried to put his arm around her shoulders but she hoisted her shoulder bag higher, holding it firmly between them.

"Foiled again," Nathaniel said jovially. "You don't have to play so hard to get, Alexa. You've definitely sparked my interest."

Alexa groaned. "How do I go about unsparking it, Nathaniel?"

"Why don't you light my fire instead, pretty woman?" Grinning confidently, he tried to slip his hand around the nape of her neck.

Alexa ducked and moved away from him, positioning herself on the other side of Tyler and Carrie. "Now he's talking in song titles," she grumbled to her sister. "Can it get any worse than this?"

"I swear Tyler and I had nothing to do with him being here," Carrie whispered earnestly. "When we asked you and Ben to come to the car show with us tonight, we didn't know that Ben would bring Nathaniel along. Honest, Alexa! I was sort of amazed you decided to come with us in the first place."

"I was bored, I wanted to get out. Going to the car show seemed like a good idea at the time." Alexa grimaced. "But if I'd known Ben was going to play matchmaker, I would've rather stayed home and watched old movies on cable. Nathaniel is such a jerk, Carrie. And he's gotten even worse since he thinks I'm harboring a secret passion for him."

Oh, how she regretted leaving that message on his answering machine. If only she hadn't let Ryan goad her into it!

"Nathaniel's a jerk but at least he's good-natured," Carrie pointed out. "Harmless too, if you don't take him seriously, and I know there's no danger of you doing that."

"Not hardly. Oh no, here he comes again." Alexa managed a polite, saccharine smile as Nathaniel joined her, chummily linking his arm with hers.

"Alexa, do you really feel like looking at all these old cars? What do you say we ditch my brother and your sibs and take off? I'll show you a real good time," Nathaniel promised, winking suggestively at her.

"Thanks but no thanks, Nathaniel." Alexa unlinked her arm from his. "I'm having a wonderful time right here."

"If you say so, babe." Nathaniel flashed his most winning smile.

Alexa caught Carrie's eye and they barely managed to stifle a giggle.

It was as if she were being held accountable for lying to Ryan about her nonexistent date tonight with Nathaniel, Alexa mused. Her punishment was an actual evening spent in Nathaniel's company, making the lie become the truth.

If she would've gone to dinner with Ryan tonight. A jolt of excitement streaked through her and Alexa sought to suppress it. She had turned down Ryan's invitation for a very good reason: because she had to stay away from him. That also meant keeping her mind off him. She'd decided to join Carrie, Tyler and Ben at the car show tonight for just that reason. If she had stayed home, she knew she would keep reliving Ryan's impromptu visit to her apartment last night. And secretly hoping that he'd show up again tonight?

The thought didn't bear considering. Rather desperately, she turned to talk with Nathaniel who assumed she was succumbing to his redoubtable charms.

"Tyler, look at that Studebaker Avanti!" Ben enthused. "Now there's a car with an awesome design *and* a V-8 engine! Whoa, wait a minute! I'm having a brainstorm! It involves filming a commercial for Tremaine Drugs right here at this car show. Wanna hear the concept, Tyler?"

"Hey, we're here to have fun not talk business," Nathaniel protested. "C'mon, let's look at that weird model over there. The one that looks like a coffin with wheels and headlights."

"That's a 1936 Cord," Tyler said reverently. "Made in Indiana. It's one of the top-ranked classic cars in the country today. Lord, I'd love to have one of those." He led the group over to the exhibition displaying three Cord convertibles.

"Daddy, Daddy, look!" the excited voice of a child sounded from the other side of the display. "Alexa is over there! See her? Let's go say hi to her."

"Sounds like you've been spotted by one of your little patients," Carrie observed, smiling at her sister. "Do you recognize the voice?"

Alexa's heart did a somersault and seemed to land upside down in her chest. She'd recognized that young voice instantly. It belonged to Kelsey Cassidy. Which meant that Ryan was here. Alexa was frozen to the spot. The often-evoked image of a deer caught in the headlights was an apt description as she stood, unable to move or make a sound, waiting for the inevitable collision.

Seconds later, Ryan pushed Kelsey in her wheelchair around the side of the Cord convertible and came face-to-face with the Shaw-Tremaine group. Alexa heard her sister gasp, watched her brother's face turn wild as a rabid bat's. Tyler was tense and unsmiling; he was aware of the antipathy between the Shaw triplets and Ryan Cassidy, had heard about Ben's sugar vendetta on his sister's behalf.

Only Nathaniel was at ease. Oblivious to the hostility and tension, he greeted Ryan with a welcoming smile and offered his hand for a hearty shake. "Ryan Cassidy!"

Nathaniel exclaimed happily. "Do you know that you're my favorite cartoonist in the entire world? And hey, you're a classic-car buff too! How've you been, my man?"

Ryan shook Nathaniel's hand but his eyes were fixed on Alexa. His initial delight at Kelsey spotting Alexa was quashed by the sight of her in Nathaniel Tremaine's company. He glanced from one to the other, incredulous. He would've bet his entire car collection that the relationship she claimed to have with Nathaniel Tremaine was a complete fabrication. But here they were together with members of her family. Sexual jealousy had been heretofore unknown to him, but he experienced it now with a ferocity that made up for lost time.

Why, she'd even dressed up for this date, Ryan noted sourly. She was wearing some sort of long black-and-red buttoned sweater and a short black pleated skirt and black stockings that displayed her long, shapely legs to sexy perfection. He felt a sharp surge of heat and a sudden leaden weight between his legs. She looked beautiful and desirable . . . and she was with another man.

He suddenly found himself unable to make the small talk the occasion required. There was a brief, awkward silence before Tyler, switching into his business-executive persona, reached for Ryan's hand, shook it and made a few pleasantries about publishing and last spring's booksellers' convention.

Ryan managed the appropriate replies; the Shaws, he noted, remained mute. The glares that Carrie and Ben directed at him were colder and more hostile than any Melissa had ever thrown his way. As for Alexa, she wasn't looking at him at all.

"Alexa, are they your other triplets?" Kelsey demanded, interrupting the boring adult dialogue between her father and Tyler to point at blond, blue-eyed Carrie and Ben. "They kinda look like you except she's shorter and he's taller."

"Yes, this is my sister Carrie and my brother Ben." Alexa's voice quavered with nervousness, instantly drawing the scrutiny of both. "I—I'd like you all to meet Kelsey Cassidy," she added.

"Hi," Kelsey said, smiling and friendly and looking so sweet, dressed all in pink, including a demure hairbow.

"Hey, Ryan, I didn't know you had a kid," Nathaniel boomed cheerfully.

"Join the club," gritted Carrie. "None of us knew."

"What happened to you, sweetie?" Nathaniel asked Kelsey, leaning down to her level. "How come you're in that wheelchair?"

"I fell off a motorcycle and got hurt," Kelsey replied. "I was in the hospital for a long time but now I'm staying at my dad's house and Alexa is my physical therapist."

"Cool," said Nathaniel.

The Nathaniel-Kelsey conversation lapsed and no new one sprang up to replace it. Alexa felt all eyes upon her. She not only read the shock and disapproval on Ben's and Carrie's faces, she could actually feel it as a tangible force.

Tyler was more sanguine about the revelation. "You didn't mention that Ryan Cassidy's child was one of your patients, Alexa," he remarked dryly. "Must've slipped your mind, hmm?"

"My dad has a car just like that one," Kelsey boasted. Seeking center stage once more, she pointed at the red '63 Corvette Stingray. "Except his is black and all scratched up. Some bad guys did it last night."

Tyler was instantly solicitous. "Your Stingray was vandalized?" He cast a furtive look at Ben, who was still scowling at Ryan. "What happened, Ryan?"

Alexa and Carrie exchanged horrified glances. It was risky to broach the subject of vandalized classic cars with Ryan, especially with Ben present.

Ryan described the damage to his Corvette. It sounded even worse than what Gloria had described. Alexa willed him not to add where the vandalism had occurred. He didn't, and she loosed a soft sigh of relief.

Tyler expressed sympathetic outrage at the car's condition, but Ben grinned maliciously.

"Wonder what you did to deserve it this time, Cassidy?" Ben speculated venomously. "You do seem to have bad luck with your collection of cars, don't you? First that '64 Thunderbird convertible of yours gets sugared and now your Stingray is used as a graffiti board." He laughed, clearly pleased with the turn of events.

Carrie and Tyler looked appalled. Alexa panicked. What if Ryan were to guess who'd done the sugaring and confront her brother with it? One glance at Ben's mutinous expression assured her that he felt no remorse for what he'd done to the car and wouldn't fake any, either.

"Interesting you should mention my old T-bird, Ben," Ryan said silkily. "Not many people knew about its demise. Even fewer knew about the sugar."

"Kelsey, would you like me to take you out to the snack bar?" Alexa suggested, her voice and her eyes unnaturally bright. "I bet you'd like a cold drink, wouldn't you? Ben, why don't you come along with us?" It was a command not an invitation. She had to get her brother out of there, away from Ryan's probing.

"Very subtle, Alexa." Ryan's eyes met hers for a moment before she quickly looked away. "But go ahead and take Kelsey. I'll join you out there shortly." His voice was so calm, so controlled, his dark eyes hooded, revealing nothing. "First, I'd like to talk to Ben."

"I want ice cream and popcorn and candy too," Kelsey announced.

"I'll go with you, lil' buddy," Nathaniel interjected. "Lead the way, Alexa."

And leave Ben and Ryan who were eyeing each other like two warring tribal chieftans? Alexa was torn and remained rooted to the spot until Nathaniel took matters into his own hands. He seized the handles of Kelsey's wheelchair and took off with her, wheeling her away.

"Come on, Alexa," Kelsey called, motioning to her.

The decision had been made for her. Now she had no choice but to go. Alexa traipsed after the pair; concern for Kelsey's welfare had to take precedence. Without proper supervision, it was all too likely that irresponsible Nathaniel might park Kelsey someplace and forget where. Ryan and Ben were adults. They would have to fend for themselves without her intervention. Anyway, Tyler and Carrie were there. They would keep things as civil as possible. Alexa gulped.

Standing amid the crowds lining up at the refreshment stands, Alexa was so rattled, she could scarcely think. Luckily she didn't have to. Nathaniel and Kelsey kept up a steady stream of chatter as Nathaniel went on a junk food spree, buying treats from every stand.

"This is more fun than looking at a bunch of dumb old cars," Kelsey proclaimed, tearing the wrapper off a giant-size chocolate bar.

"You've got that right," Nathaniel agreed, chomping on an ice-cream bar. "Hey, here comes your dad."

Alexa's head whipped around to see Ryan striding toward them. "Ready to go, Kelsey?" he asked briskly.

Kelsey clutched her tub of popcorn, her plastic cup of ice cream, industrial-size soda and candy bars. "I'm not done eating yet," she protested.

"You can take the stuff with you and eat it on the way home," her father promised. "It's definitely time for us to leave."

Ryan hadn't even glanced her way, Alexa noted nervously. Having experienced his constant attention these past few days, she realized how accustomed she'd become to having him focus on her, to seeing his eyes, intent and intense, watch her every move. Up until this very moment, she would've maintained that she loathed his scrutiny, that she didn't want to encourage his interest. But now . . .

She couldn't take her eyes off him. His coffee-brown chambray shirt heightened the color of his eyes, and of course, nobody wore jeans better than Ryan Cassidy. Long-legged, slim-hipped, unmistakably all virile male. And he was totally ignoring her.

"Ryan, how did it go with Ben?" she blurted out.

She felt the full force of his dark gaze upon her now. Alexa's cheeks flushed. Heaven help her, she liked his attention, she wanted it. And it seemed she would say anything to get it. *How did it go with Ben?* Was she crazy?

"Why don't you ask him?" Ryan replied cryptically.

"Well, I—I—" She swallowed not knowing what to say, wondering what, if anything, had been revealed.

"It's getting late." Ryan cast a perfunctory glance at his watch. "Say good-night to everyone, Kelsey." He pushed her wheelchair away as Kelsey bellowed a boisterous good-night.

Instinctively, automatically, Alexa rushed after them. "Ryan, wait!"

He paused, watching her approach, his lips tightened in a firm straight line. He said nothing, waiting for her to speak first.

She swallowed. "You're leaving, just like that? Without saying a word?"

"There are a lot of things I could say but—" he glanced at Kelsey who was gobbling down her treats "—my child is here. I want to take her home."

"And—and then begin to plot strategy?" Alexa tried to sound cool and confident with just a touch of glib charm thrown in. She had a strong feeling she'd failed utterly.

"Good night, Alexa," Ryan said and left with Kelsey.

Alexa watched them disappear into the crowd. Was it her imagination or had his good-night sounded chillingly like a final goodbye? Because he now knew what Ben had done and wanted no part of anyone connected with such deeds? Because he was already planning his own revenge? She stood worried and bereft while Nathaniel blathered on and on about the merits of one brand of beer over another.

They were still standing there, Nathaniel talking and Alexa lost in thought and not listening, when Carrie, Tyler and Ben joined them.

"I've finally figured it out. Kelsey Cassidy is the patient with the little brother and the battling parents, isn't she, Alexa?" Carrie exclaimed, her blue eyes wide with comprehension. "You took Franklin and Emily to Ryan's house to help arrange Kelsey's little brother's visit."

"I make one obscure remark about sugar and Cassidy puts it all together," Ben intoned glumly. "Somehow he figured out that *I* was the one who put the sugar in the gas tank of the T-bird and smuggled the pigeons inside his house and ordered those hundred pizzas to be delivered to his address and made all those bogus pledges to telethons in his name and—"

"You did all that?" Nathaniel looked impressed.

"And more," Ben added, brightening a little from Nathaniel's approval. "I put his phone number in a personal ad, requesting raunchy sex, in dozens of raunchy sex magazines, both straight and gay. I bet he got kinky callers around the clock for weeks! I ordered tons of stuff in his name from those TV offers—everything from tapes to tools—and had them sent COD to his address." He paused. "Mmm, I know there's some other things but I can't think of them right off the bat. After all, it's been two years since I launched my—er—campaign."

"Never mind, Ben," Carrie warned. "I think you've said enough."

"Wow, what an operative you are, Ben!" Nathaniel exclaimed admiringly. "Have you ever thought about working in a political campaign? You'd be a natural in the dirty-tricks division."

"A new career path for him to consider after he gets out of jail," Tyler said acidly. "Cassidy was furious and I don't blame him. I knew about the car and thought that was terrible enough, but all this stuff about the pigeons and pizzas and pledges and the—"

"He can't send Ben to jail!" Carrie cut in anxiously. "All of those things happened two years ago. Isn't there a statute of limitations or something?"

"If there is, I'm sure Ben's attorney will let him know," Tyler gritted. "And that attorney will not be associated in any way with Tremaine Incorporated." He eyed Ben sternly. "You're on your own with this. Do I make myself clear?"

Ben nodded, uncharacteristically solemn.

"We can't turn our backs on Ben!" Carrie looked ready to cry. "Benjy, don't worry. You know that if you need our help, we'll do everything possible to—"

"Don't make promises you won't be able to keep, Carrie," Tyler said firmly. "*Benjy* is an adult and is fully responsible for the consequences of his own actions."

"Not that old lecture!" Nathaniel groaned. "I've only heard it a few billion times myself from my father and all my brothers. Pay my big brother no mind, Ben. Sometimes his sense of humor is sorely lacking."

"In this case, it most certainly is," Tyler growled. "Come on, Carrie. We're leaving."

"We can't go yet," Carrie cried. Her eyes connected frantically with Alexa's. "Especially not under these circumstances."

Alexa felt a sinking sensation in the pit of her stomach; she acutely felt her sister's distress as well as her own. She tried to fix things for Carrie. "Tyler, try to understand. This isn't a loyalty test," Alexa hastened to explain.

"Good thing it isn't 'cause you'd probably lose, Tyler," Nathaniel chortled. "I mean, Carrie's been a triplet with Ben and Alexa for twenty-seven years. She's only been married to you for one. Blood's thicker than water, you know. At least, that's what Dad's always yammering about."

Tyler dismissed his younger brother with an exasperated scowl. He held out his hand to Carrie. "We're going home, Carrie. Now."

Carrie stood between Alexa and Ben and didn't move.

"Showdown!" Nathaniel exclaimed gleefully.

"No, it's not," Alexa countered. She lowered her voice, out of earshot of the Tremaine brothers. Her remarks were for her siblings only. "We have to think, we can't panic."

"Not panic?" cried Carrie. "Alexa, you don't know how mad Ryan was! You weren't there when he was talking to Ben. He looked like he was going to choke him on the spot. We all know how heartless Ryan Cassidy is—he proved it by the way he treated you, Alexa! And now he's going to hurt Ben! He's going to press charges and he has friends in high places. He'll see to it that Ben's thrown in prison or sue him for every cent he'll ever make, and if the Tremaines won't help, we won't have a chance against him!"

"Now, wait a minute. Ryan is not the almighty ogre you think he is," Alexa interjected. This conversation had an almost familiar ring to it, except the last time she'd had it, Melissa had been the one speculating on Ryan's heinous plans and powers. Melissa had been wrong; hopefully Carrie was too.

"Don't tell me you've fallen back under Cassidy's spell!" Ben squawked. "Alexa, how can you trust the guy? He—he's a demon!"

"He's not a demon because he broke up with me," Alexa said quietly. "I appreciate your loyalty but you overreacted back then, Ben. You were way out of line, and I'm sorry I waited until now to say it."

"He's brainwashed you already!" Ben moaned. "Carrie, talk some sense into your sister!"

"Uh-oh, there's trouble in paradise." Nathaniel broke into the trio. "Tyler's taking off, and he doesn't look happy."

The triplets turned to see Tyler striding toward the doors of the arena. Carrie ran after him without a moment's hesitation or backward glance.

"Oh, the fight they're going to have!" Nathaniel predicted, grinning. "I bet it'll register an earthshaking ten on the Richter scale."

"I don't want them to fight!" Ben was visibly perturbed. "I'm going after them. I can smooth things over, take the blame..." He took off after them at breakneck speed.

"Ben will do anything to protect his job with the company, huh?" Nathaniel observed cynically. "He values the Tremaine name more than I do."

Alexa glared at him. "Ben is worried about more than his job with Tremaine Incorporated. He's genuinely concerned for Carrie, just the way he was concerned for me after Ryan and I broke up." She heaved a doleful sigh. "Which is how this entire mess started. Now Tyler and Carrie are fighting and Ben is in trouble. And I have to make things right. I'm the only one who can do it."

"Going to get down on your knees and beg Cassidy for mercy?" Nathaniel laughed wickedly. "I recommend wearing only a garter belt, stockings and high heels when you do. It just might even the odds against you."

Alexa's face burned. "You're disgusting, Nathaniel."

"Hey, lighten up. I'm just trying to inject a little humor into the situation. Want a ride home?"

"Since my family has disappeared, leaving me rideless, I'm afraid I have no choice but to accept your offer."

"My offer comes with a condition, babe. I'll drive you home only if you agree to go out with me tomorrow night."

Alexa stifled an impatient sigh. "All right, I will." It was an engagement she had no intention of keeping. As if she would honor a date made under duress! But right now she would agree to almost anything to get out of here.

When they were ensconced in Nathaniel's Ferrari, he asked for directions to her place. Alexa found herself directing him to Ryan's house instead. She had no specific

plan in mind but she knew she had to talk to Ryan tonight.
After all, both Carrie's and Ben's happiness depended on it.
Her brother's future would be wrecked if he were jailed or
sued, and if Tyler refused to help Ben, Carrie would be at
odds with him. The thought of Carrie and Tyler's marriage
turning sour chilled Alexa. She couldn't allow that to happen, not any of it!

Nathaniel turned on his CD player and music filled the
car with pulsing primitive drumbeats and a sensually husky
voice singing lyrics that were sexy and evocative.

Alexa felt wired and high-strung, her heart pounding
along with the drums. And though she'd undertaken this
mission for the sake of Carrie and Ben, it was not them she
thought of as they sped through the night.

The thoughts tumbling through her mind, interspersed
with a kaleidoscope of visual images, were all of Ryan Cassidy. There were scenes from both the past and the present,
and they ran the gamut from conversations and arguments
to tender love scenes and hot passionate sex.

Juxtaposing those scenes, a stunning realization slowly
began to dawn. Had she and Ryan dealt with each other as
openly and honestly two years ago as they did today,
chances were good that their breakup would not have occurred. But she had been insecure and uncertain, and Ryan
had been defensive and evasive. Neither had really trusted
the other. Ryan had kept his secrets from her, and she hadn't
been experienced or forthright enough to understand and
command complete honesty.

And now . . . Alexa thought of Ryan's cool dismissal this
evening, how he'd whisked Kelsey away, barricading himself behind the enigmatic, imperturbable facade he used to
keep others at bay. Two years ago she'd let him shut her out.
She wasn't going to let it happen again tonight.

Alexa, how can you trust the guy? Ben's words rang in her
ears. Until this moment, she hadn't realized that she did.
Now she knew. Ryan had proved to her that he could deal
fairly with Melissa, that he was willing to consider Kelsey's

best interests above his own wishes. She trusted him to keep his word in those matters; somehow she was absolutely certain that he would.

So if she could trust him, did that mean she could love him again?

"You haven't heard a word I've said," Nathaniel complained.

The sound of his voice startled Alexa so much she jumped. She flushed, embarrassed. She'd been so preoccupied with her own thoughts and insights, she'd forgotten Nathaniel's very existence.

"Whew, you're murder on a guy's ego." Nathaniel grimaced. "I mean, there's such a thing as playing hard to get but you carry it to extremes!"

"I'm sorry, Nathaniel," Alexa said contritely. "I've been rude to ignore you. What were you saying? I promise I'll listen this time."

"Never mind," Nathaniel grumbled. "I'm finally coming to the conclusion that you're not playing hard to get, after all. You're just plain not interested. There's somebody else, right? You're in love with some other guy."

Alexa stared silently ahead. Was she in love with Ryan? Had she ever stopped loving him in the first place? "I don't know, Nathaniel," she murmured.

But she did know.

And she couldn't have chosen a worse time to finally admit her love for Ryan, Alexa decided gloomily. Tonight's revelation of revenge had evoked his fury. Frustrated and discouraged, her eyes filled with tears. When Ryan had professed his love for her, she'd denied hers for him, genuinely believing her own denial. Would they ever get their timing right?

Nathaniel swung the powerful sports car into the long, tree-lined driveway. "Hey, where are we anyway?" he demanded. "I thought you lived in an apartment complex in some ugly suburban sprawl."

"We're at a—a friend's house. You can just drop me off here, Nathaniel. And thanks so much for the ride."

Nathaniel braked the car to a stop a few feet away from the grand entranceway. "You don't want me to wait around in case Cassidy kicks you out? He might, you know. What your brother did to his prized car is no small thing to a dedicated collector, Alexa. And all those other dirty tricks could put a definite damper on any romance."

His thoughts echoed her own, and her spirits sank even lower. "I'm only here to..." Alexa's voice trailed off. She couldn't find the right words, and even if she could, she wasn't about to confide in Nathaniel Tremaine.

"You're a mixed-up, shook-up girl," Nathaniel observed, amused.

"Uh-oh, you're talking in song titles again. My cue to leave." Alexa opened the car door and climbed out.

"I guess I can forget about our date tomorrow night?"

Alexa nodded her head. "Sorry, Nathaniel."

He shrugged. "It's just as well. You come with too many strings attached, and I'm not about to get tied down."

"Thanks for being a good sport about it, Nathaniel." She gave him a quick smile and a wave before turning to head toward the imposing front door.

Her heart was racing as she lifted the heavy brass knocker and sounded it twice. A few seconds passed and she knocked again, apprehension and anticipation churning through her, so intermixed she couldn't separate one from the other.

The door swung open and Ryan stood before her. His face was an unreadable mask, offering no clues as to whether she was welcome or an anathema. Alexa's eyes swept over him. He stood rigid and tense, his hands balled into fists, his dark eyes burning into her.

She fought the sudden, cowardly urge to turn and run. Nathaniel's car was still idling in front of the mansion. She could be in it within seconds and on her way home, away from the risk of Ryan's censure, safe from the pain of his rejection.

She'd spent the past two years avoiding emotional risk and shielding herself from pain. She could do it again....

Instead she took a deep breath, squared her shoulders and met his gaze directly. "Are you going to invite me in or keep me standing out here like a bill collector?"

Ten

—

"Kelsey is in bed for the night," Ryan said coolly. "If you've come to see her, you've made a wasted trip."

Alexa's nerves were taut and on edge. So this was the way he was going to play it? He knew very well that she wasn't here in her professional capacity to visit Kelsey. Having experienced Ben's campaign of vengeance, it seemed Ryan Cassidy was now indulging in a bit of revenge himself.

Her mouth tightened. "I'm not here to see Kelsey. I've come to talk to you, Ryan."

"I see. I take it you're here to plead brother Ben's case?" Ryan's eyes swept past her and lingered for a moment on Nathaniel's car. "Is the boyfriend going to wait while you do?"

"Nathaniel isn't my boyfriend." Alexa met and held his gaze. He was still blocking the door and made no move to let her inside.

"No? But you made such an effort to convince me that he was."

"It was a wasted effort. You didn't believe me anyway." She folded her arms in front of her, frowning. "I'm not going to stand out here and spar with you, Ryan. I'll leave if you want me to."

She wasn't going to humble herself and beg him for his time, for his attention or anything else! She hadn't done so two years ago, when he'd driven her away. She'd gone quietly and he hadn't tried to stop her. He hadn't come after her, either, though now he claimed he'd been miserable without her.

Alexa studied the firm set of his jaw and his glittering dark eyes. Ryan seemed as unreachable now as he had back then, when his withdrawal from her had broken her heart.

Nathaniel chose that moment to rev his engine and peel out of the driveway like a race car in the final heat of the Indy 500.

"Uh-oh, looks like your ride has left. Too bad," Ryan taunted. "Now you're stuck here."

"No, I'm not." She inclined her head defiantly. One thing she'd learned since Ryan had reentered her life was that she could now hold her own with him. And that two could play his evasive games. "I can always call myself a taxi."

"Of course you can. There's a phone booth a few miles down the road, at the service station."

"Yes, I saw it on our way here. Luckily it's a beautiful night for a walk." Her head held high, Alexa turned and started down the porch steps.

"Wouldn't you be shocked if I called your bluff and didn't insist that you come back here?" Ryan followed her but remained several paces behind her.

By choice, Alexa knew. A few swift, long-legged strides and he could easily catch up to her. If he wanted to. If. Alexa steeled herself against raising any false hopes. Still, he was following her, he hadn't gone inside and let her walk away...

"Wouldn't *you* be shocked if I walked the entire way to the phone booth and called the taxi?" she retorted.

"Yeah, I would." Ryan stopped and stood at the foot of the wide porch stairs. "It won't do your brother Ben any good if you made me any madder than I already am, Alexa."

Alexa kept on walking. "I don't respond to threats," she called over her shoulder.

"You don't respond to threats, but you do like to make them, don't you, Alexa?"

The baiting challenge in his tone stopped her in her tracks, but she kept her back to him. "I don't make threats," she said disdainfully.

"No? What about the way you kept threatening me with the almighty power of the Tremaines? Not that it worked. I knew all along you were bluffing."

She whirled round to face him. "The way you're bluffing now? Do you want to talk about what Ben, about what went on back then or not, Ryan?"

"Why don't you come inside and we'll discuss it?"

She watched him return to the front door, which was still standing partially ajar. A rush of adrenaline poured through her as the fight-or-flight response was activated. Should she go inside for the confrontation? Or run away to safety? And if she were to leave, would he come after her? He'd let her go before and stayed away for two long, lonely years.

"Alexa," Ryan's voice sounded from the porch where he stood watching her. "Come here."

She stopped thinking, stopped analyzing, and acted on pure reckless impulse. "On second thought, I think I'll go. You can discuss your course of action with Ben's attorney."

The blood roaring in her ears, her pulses racing, she turned and marched grandly down the driveway.

Moments later Ryan was beside her, his fingers fastening around her wrist to bring her to an abrupt, cartoon-style halt. "Let's try this again, shall we? I'll say, 'Come inside with me, Alexa.' And you'll say..." He paused expectantly.

"What if I don't say anything?" she challenged, her tone, her stance and her big blue eyes provocative. "What if I just keep on walking, Ryan?"

"Try it and see how far you get," he suggested silkily.

Her eyes clashed with his, then she turned and began walking. And managed to get only an arm's length away from him. Her wrist was still securely manacled by his fingers' viselike grip.

"Hmm, not very far." Ryan smiled, a slow sexual grin that sent shivers of response along her spine. "You're coming with me, Alexa." His voice was soft but tinged with masculine roughness. His smoldering dark eyes radiated heat. "You can either walk or I'll fling you over my shoulder and carry you. Your choice."

Alexa cleared her throat. "I prefer to walk," she said with dignity. But it was strictly a facade. Her stomach was fluttering; she was light-headed yet her limbs felt languorously heavy.

Ryan released her wrist, but his fingers slipped lower to interlace with hers. They walked back to the house together in silence, her hand clasped in his big warm one.

In the doorway Ryan turned slightly aside, allowing her only minimum space to pass through, guaranteeing that she would have to brush by him. When she did, both of them felt the power of the contact.

Alexa's whole body reacted to the touch of his as waves of fiery sexual heat surged through her. They stood together for a moment, crowded in the doorway, her wide blue eyes locked with his dark, restless ones. They were so close she could feel his warm breath against her lips, and it called forth sizzling memories of the hard pressure of his mouth upon hers, the sublime feel of their lips and tongues meeting, caressing.

"Did Ben ask you to come over here?" Ryan asked at last, breaking the charged silence.

Alexa blinked. "What?" She sounded dazed. Her own erotic reminiscences, coupled with the way he was looking at her, shattered every coherent thought.

"Ben," Ryan repeated patiently. "You remember him. Your brother. The devil in disguise." He was enjoying the fact that he could unsettle her with simply a look, that she was visibly affected by their proximity.

Alexa knew it. Trembling, she quickly moved away from him to stand in the cavernous vestibule. She watched Ryan close the door. And lock it, sliding the bolt firmly into place.

She drew in a deep breath. "Ben didn't ask me to come. I—I wanted to apologize to you on his behalf. I know what he did was awful but—"

"You wanted revenge and your brother made sure you got it," Ryan finished for her. He was standing in front of her now, his body hot and hard.

"No! I didn't know what Ben was doing until after he'd done it. Neither did Carrie. When we found out we were horrified. We told him to stop." She stared at him, her blue eyes perceptive. "You thought I was in on the whole thing, didn't you? That not only did I approve, I might've even initiated it and helped Ben carry everything out."

"That possibility did cross my mind."

"Which explains why you bolted from the car show and looked at me like I was the felon-of-the-week on *America's Most Wanted.*"

"I wanted to get Kelsey out of there. I fully intended to— uh—talk things over with you later on, but it took me a while to assimilate the fact that I finally knew the origin of that particular string of incidents."

"Particular string of incidents," Alexa repeated softly. "You'd call that a euphemistic whitewash in your strip. And follow it up with a satire on doublespeak."

"Back then, I thought everything that was happening was a result of my strip." Ryan grimaced. "I assumed I was the target of some zealous group of fanatics that I'd offended. I kept waiting for their letters to arrive claiming credit and demanding that I change my storyline or write one that espoused their particular views. And all the time, it was your brother Ben."

"Ben can be—uh—zealous, especially when it involves Carrie and me. He's zealous about his ambitions, too," she added, troubled but truthful.

"Ben was furious with me for hurting you," Ryan said flatly.

Alexa nodded, averting her eyes. "But I didn't want revenge, Ryan. I just wanted..." Her voice trailed off.

"What did you want, Alexa?" he asked quietly.

"You," she whispered, staring at the plushly carpeted floor. "I wanted you back."

"And now?" he pressed. "Do you still want me back, Alexa? Or did you really mean it when you said you didn't love me anymore?"

She ran a nervous hand through her hair. "I thought I meant it when I said it."

"I thought I meant it when I told you I didn't want to be seriously involved with you. And for two unbearably long, unhappy years I've lived with the consequences of those words."

"Those consequences being Ben's nasty tricks?"

"I was referring to being without you, not to Ben's misdeeds." Ryan smiled grimly. "Can we quit the verbal fencing, Alexa? Be straight with me. Do you want me back or don't you?"

She flushed. She was afraid, she realized. What if Ryan was laying a trap for her, getting her to admit that she still loved him so he could have the opportunity to reject her all over again? It would certainly be a neat revenge for all the vengeful acts Ben had pulled on him. The things Ben had done were reprehensible; it wasn't outside the realm of possibility that Ryan found them unforgivable. And wasn't there some chilling admonition about vengeance begetting vengeance? Or something along those lines.

Alexa looked up at him, breathless. She'd realized on the drive over here that she loved Ryan. And love was so bound up in trust that one couldn't exist without the other. So if she loved him, she had to trust him not to hurt her again. He'd done it before and he'd told her how much he regretted it.

If they were to ever have a future together, she would have to put the hurt behind her and wipe the slate clean. To give him another chance. To trust him.

Her blue eyes were bright with emotion. "I want you back, Ryan," she said achingly. "I love you, I've never stopped. Even when I thought I hated you, I loved you. So if you still want me—"

"If?" He moved like lightning, cupping his hands beneath her bottom and lifting her up. Automatically she wrapped her legs around his hips and her arms around his neck. Her skirt slid to her thighs and her breasts nestled against his chest. Ryan closed his eyes as a potent rush of desire and urgent need nearly buckled his knees. He held her tighter, grasping her more securely.

"I want you, baby," he rasped. "So much that I want to put the past behind us, to forget our breakup and Ben's revenge and get on with our life together. I love you, Alexa. I don't want you to ever doubt that again. I intend to spend the rest of my life making sure you don't."

She drew back her head a little to gaze into his eyes. "That—sounds like a proposal," she dared to say.

"That's because it is a proposal. One that's two years overdue." He touched his mouth to hers, his lips teasing and tempting. "Say yes, Alexa. Say you'll marry me. We've already wasted too much time."

She stared at him. *A marriage proposal?* "I'm having trouble assimilating this, Ryan."

"Maybe this will help." His lips brushed hers in a featherlight caress, back and forth, over and over, until Alexa was desperate for the hard hungry pressure of his mouth.

She whimpered when he pressed his open mouth against her neck, nibbling with his teeth, then laving the sensitive skin with his tongue. Alexa ran her hands over the rippling muscles in his back, tilting her head back to allow him greater access. His strong arms held her securely, anchored against him. Slowly, sensually, his hands slipped beneath her skirt, skimming along the nylon-clad length of her thighs, to knead the rounded softness of her bottom.

Alexa tightened her legs around him, grinding her hips against the thickness of his burgeoning masculinity. He was hard and unyielding against her complementing softness, and the elemental contrast electrified them both.

Their mouths met and melded, his tongue penetrating deep into her moist warmth, tantalizing her tongue and drawing it into his own mouth, then returning to hers to probe every sweet hollow. The kiss grew deeper and deeper, more urgent and intimate and passionate.

When they finally broke apart for breath, they were both panting. Their faces were flushed, their bodies on fire with an urgent yearning and a fierce lust.

"How's the assimilation coming along?" Ryan's voice was husky, his coffee-brown eyes gleaming. "I'll be glad to provide whatever further assistance is needed to speed up the process."

"Oh, Ryan," Alexa whispered.

Her body was one heated throb. Clinging to him, she touched her lips against the hard, tanned column of his neck. Her nipples were tight and straining and aching to be touched. She rubbed them softly against his chest, seeking the pressure to soothe the sensual ache. He was hard and thick between her legs and she squirmed against him, feeling swollen and achy, wanting, needing him to fill the throbbing emptiness within her.

"You haven't said you'll marry me yet," Ryan reminded her.

Alexa unlocked her legs and slid slowly to her feet, Ryan's arms keeping her arched against the long length of his body. She had to cling to him for support, for her limbs were wobbly and weak, her breathing shallow and erratic.

She gazed up at him, her eyes cloudy with passion. "I want to marry you, Ryan."

"Sweetheart!" He crushed her to him. "You've made me the happiest man in the world, Alexa," he said fervently.

"I'm happy too, Ryan," she whispered. "I—I can hardly believe that we're finally back together."

"You see, I was right," Ryan said rather smugly. "We're back together, and just so we're both on the same wavelength this time, 'back together' means that we're definitely a couple. A couple who love each other and are committed to each other."

"And who also have great sex," Alexa teased.

She felt so happy, as if a great weight had been lifted from her heart. She was free, unburdened from the confusion and misery and doubt that had plagued her. A bolstering surge of certainty sent her confidence soaring.

"I think it's time we enjoyed some of that great sex right now," Ryan said, flashing a wicked grin. "Spend the night with me, Alexa."

"I want to. But what about Kelsey and Gloria?"

"They've both turned in for the night. My room is far enough away from both of theirs to ensure us complete privacy." He swung her up in his arms and carried her up the stairs in time-honored, romantic fashion, not the fireman's carry he'd threatened outside.

His bedroom was a revelation. Alexa burst out laughing at the sight of it. "Nadine outdid herself on this room." She gazed around, grinning. "It's the jungle primeval in here. All you need are vines and Cheetah to experience the thrill of being Tarzan and Jane."

"I'm putting this place on the market immediately," Ryan declared. "I have no intention of living in a comic-strip set that sends my bride-to-be into fits of laughter in the middle of what's supposed to be an intensely passionate scene."

"We'll get right back to the intensely passionate scene," Alexa promised. "But I do like the idea of not having to live here. I'd like a more—uh—traditional home."

"A place Nadine didn't decorate," Ryan suggested.

"A place big enough for you and me and for your studio," Alexa said dreamily, toying with his belt buckle. "And of course, we'll need a room for Kelsey for when she visits us." Her fingers slid to the button fly of his jeans. Ryan groaned and held her hand against him for a moment before lifting it to kiss each of her fingertips.

"What about the twins or the triplets we'll probably have? We'll need plenty of space for them. Maybe we'll have a set of each."

"You won't mind dealing with another generation of littermates?" she teased.

"I'm looking forward to it." He unfastened the first button of her sweater and leaned down to kiss the hollow of her throat. Alexa moaned and arched her back, touching her stomach to his.

Ryan undid the next three buttons, his lips trailing a path along her smooth skin. With the sweater half-opened, her breasts were exposed to him, full and white and swelling out of the lacy cups of her low-cut bra. Her nipples, raised and pink, jutted against the sheer lace.

Ryan groaned in sheer pleasure at the feminine sight. He laid a hand over each breast, cupping them possessively, his palms pressing against the taut centers. Reflexively she clutched his shoulders for support. Her grip tightened as Ryan unclasped her bra and slipped it off along with her sweater. When he kissed first one nipple, then the other, her fingernails dug into him and she swayed dizzily from sheer sensation.

"I think it's time to lie down," Ryan said huskily, guiding her to the king-size bed. He sat on the edge and pulled her down onto his lap. His arms encircled her waist and he nuzzled her neck. "I'm so glad you're here with me, Alexa," he said with a heartfelt sincerity that brought tears to her eyes.

"I love you, Ryan." She laid her head on his shoulder, her hands linked with his, and for a moment the two of them were content to hold each other and savor their closeness.

But the passion between them was too strong to go unslaked for long. When Ryan took her mouth, she responded with helpless, mindless urgency. He kissed her deeply, possessively, their desire and need building and burning hotter and higher.

Suddenly their clothes were a frustrating impediment that neither could tolerate, and they shed them with dizzying speed, each helping the other.

They lay down together, stretching out on the big bed. Ryan's dark eyes watched Alexa, studying every curve and line of her body, and his unconcealed ardor and admiration sent a flood of hot honeyed warmth through her.

She trembled as his hands moved purposefully over the sensitive peaks of her breasts, then replaced them with his lips, drawing first one and then the other into the wet warmth of his mouth.

Ryan smiled hotly when she moaned and arched up to him. "I want to kiss you everywhere, Alexa. Here and here..." His mouth caressed her nipples, then moved to her navel, teasing the small hollow with his tongue. "I want to kiss every inch of you, my baby."

Alexa was on fire. A wild little cry escaped from her throat as he kissed a path from her belly to the softness of her moist feminine heat. Lightning streaks of sensation, more powerful than any she'd ever experienced before, skyrocketed through her body. She shimmered on the edge of rapturous pleasure as his sweet kisses sent her into a mindless, freefall. She gasped his name as exquisite waves of pure ecstasy flooded through her.

He didn't give her time to come down. With a low, sexy growl, Ryan covered her body with his, smoothly, masterfully surging into her warm center. Alexa welcomed him with a passionate, enveloping shudder.

"I love you," she cried, wrapping herself around him as he moved within her. This was so much more than sex, this was love that transcended the physical pleasure they gave to each other. She'd been lying to herself when she'd tried to deny it. She and Ryan belonged together; the love they shared was elemental and right.

"Come with me, Alexa," Ryan said hoarsely. "Come with me now, love."

She gave herself over to him completely, surrendering to the power of their love. They clasped hands on either side of her head, their fingers locked tightly, as their passion broke into stormy crests of rapture, dissolving into a shattering mutual release.

They held on to each other for long after the climax had subsided, warm and languid in the sensual afterglow.

Finally Alexa, relaxed and thoroughly sated, stretched beneath him. Ryan lifted his head and gazed into her eyes. They smiled lovingly at each other.

"I guess we have a wedding date to set," said Ryan, shifting his weight to tuck her against him, spoon-fashion.

"Mmm, how about in the spring? That will give us plenty of time to—"

"But that's months from now," Ryan protested. "I was thinking more along the lines of next week."

Alexa turned to face him, cuddling close. "I like the idea of being engaged. Of having enough time to plan a beautiful wedding. It's the only one I intend to have, you know."

Ryan gave her a slow, assessing look. "Are you sure that's the reason why you want to wait? Or are you still not sure you trust me not to hurt you again? Do you need more time for me to prove that I can be counted on to stick around?"

"I know I love you, and I know I want to marry you, Ryan." Alexa touched his cheek. "But there is no need to rush into anything, not unless you have doubts."

It was Ryan's turn to interrupt. "I have no doubts that I'm crazy about you and that I want to spend the rest of my life with you." His voice was husky and his eyes were dark with emotion. "And if you want to wait until spring to be married, I'll just have to grin and bear it because I'm in your life to stay, sweetie."

Alexa lifted her face to kiss him tenderly. "There are other reasons why I'd like to wait a few months, Ryan. One of them is Kelsey. I'd like her to be much further along in her convalescence when we're married. I want her to be in our wedding and to see her walk down the aisle."

"And you think she'll be able to do that in the spring?" Ryan dared to hope.

Alexa nodded. "She's showing very encouraging signs of progress. But she needs more intensive treatment than what she's getting here, Ryan. And keeping her isolated here is not helping her socially and educationally, I think you know that."

"You're recommending the Children's Rehabilitation Institute?"

Alexa nodded. "It's a first-rate place. I guarantee she'll do well there in every way. Which brings us to Melissa . . ."

Ryan groaned in protest. "We're not going to talk about *her,* not here, not now. She'll revel in the fact that I've agreed to send Kelsey to that institute but—"

"I think you should increase your child-support payments," Alexa said. "Kelsey is getting older and her needs are more costly. Melissa and Jack are having a very difficult time financially, and for Kelsey's sake, we should help them out."

Ryan gaped at her. "Good God, I'm marrying my ex-wife's advocate! Alexa, you don't understand what she—"

Alexa cupped his face in her hands and gazed deeply into his dark eyes. "I understand that you're a loving father who wants to do what's best for your child. And I also understand that your hostility toward Melissa sometimes gets in the way of that. You and Melissa have got to stop being adversaries, for—"

"Kelsey's sake," Ryan chimed in. He took her hands, kissing both palms.

"When it comes to Kelsey, we're all on the same side, Ryan."

"Well, I know Kelsey will be pleased that we're getting married," said Ryan. "She really likes you, Alexa. I only wish your sister and brother didn't hate my guts, although I fully understand why they do. Think they'll ever be able to forgive me for hurting you?"

"I'm sure they will," Alexa said warmly. "We'll spend time with them, they can get to know you all over again and—oh no!" She bolted upright, gasping. "Carrie and Tyler! They argued at the car show and both of them went storming out. I've got to call Carrie and tell her not to worry about Ben's fate. Maybe then she can work things out with Tyler. I hope it's not too late!''

Resignedly Ryan handed her the phone. Her heart was pounding as she pressed the numbers. What if their quarrel had turned so ugly that neither Carrie nor Tyler could forgive and forget? It would be heartbreakingly ironic if her sister's life were to fall apart just as her own romance was finally, finally working out.

There were two short rings and Tyler breathed into the phone, "This better be important." His voice was thick and deep and husky. He sounded strange...

"Tyler, did—did I call at a bad time?" Alexa asked uncertainly.

"No, Alexa, you called in the middle of a very good time." On the other end of the line, Tyler was chuckling. "Do you want to talk to Carrie? She's the one I'm having the good time with."

Carrie was on the line within seconds. She'd obviously been standing right beside her husband—or lying beside him? Alexa thought of the phone on the nightstand right next to the bed in her sister's bedroom.

"I thought I'd call to tell you that Ben won't be needing an attorney and to try to save your marriage to Tyler," Alexa said wryly.

"Save my marriage?" Carrie echoed incredulously. "Oh, Alexa, Tyler and I just had a little spat tonight. We do, periodically. It doesn't mean we're going to break up. We love each other, Alexa. I only wish you could believe that love doesn't have to end in misery and revenge."

Alexa looked up at Ryan and smiled. "I do believe it, Carrie. And I also believe that loving is the best revenge of all."

Eleven

Seven months later, on a sunny Saturday in May, Alexa Shaw and Ryan Cassidy were married. The Tremaine triplets, Dylan, Emily and Franklin, were the first members of the wedding party to walk down the aisle of the church and they went down as a threesome.

Emily, the flower girl, resplendent in ruffles and ribbons and shiny patent leather shoes, walked between her two brothers, clutching a small basket of rose petals that she refused to scatter.

Dylan's and Franklin's roles were not quite defined, other than accompanying Emily and looking adorable in their toddler-size white suits. The trio evoked a chorus of oohs and ahhs as they paraded down the aisle, and Tyler, their proud daddy, beamed as he gathered them into the pew beside him.

Next came junior bridesmaid, Kelsey, wearing the long purple dress she'd personally selected. She carried a nosegay of purple flowers and walked slowly and carefully but straight and unassisted, unaided by any supportive therapy equipment. She smiled and nodded graciously at the guests as she passed down the aisle, giggling when Nathaniel Tremaine gave her an enthusiastic thumbs-up.

Carrie Tremaine, Alexa's matron of honor, was to follow Kelsey, but before she started down the aisle, she fussed with Alexa's veil one last time and dabbed at her eyes with the handkerchief her father, Colonel Shaw in full dress uniform, thoughtfully supplied.

"You look beautiful, Alexa," Carrie whispered, her eyes refilling with emotional tears as quickly as she wiped them away. "I'm so happy for you and for Ryan, too. He's perfect for you, Alexa. In every way."

Alexa squeezed her sister's hand. These past seven months had confirmed to everybody who knew them what Alexa and Ryan already knew—that they were absolutely and unquestionably right for each other.

Even Melissa had warmly wished Alexa happiness, though she remained less effusive toward Ryan. But the hostility between Ryan and Melissa was mellowing, particularly since she'd married Jack Webber three months ago. Jack was now working at one of the Tremaine Drugstores distribution centers and maintained a friendly relationship with Alexa and a civil one with Ryan. Kelsey lived with her mother, brother and stepfather and visited Ryan regularly. She took full credit for her father's engagement to Alexa and boasted of her incredible matchmaking powers. Neither Ryan nor Alexa saw any reason to disabuse her of the notion that she'd brought the two of them together. In a roundabout way, she had!

"Both my girls married! Imagine that!" Colonel Shaw marveled, smiling fondly at his daughters. "And you've both married very well." His smile widened and he looked startlingly like his son Ben. "Very well indeed. Now if only your brother would settle down with a nice girl..."

"I don't think Ben's ready for marriage just yet, Daddy," Carrie said dryly.

"It's sort of terrifying to imagine the woman who will make a husband out of Ben," Alexa murmured. "She'll have to be a Machiavellian trickster with a scholarly understanding of revenge.''

''Well, I hope you two will be as warm and welcoming to whomever Ben marries as he's been to Tyler and Ryan,'' stated Colonel Shaw. ''Your brother thinks the world of those two. Thinks of them as his own blood brothers.''

Alexa and Carrie looked at each other. It was true that Ben was high on both his sisters' mates these days. And there were other, certain things best forgotten.

The musical cue sounded and Carrie floated serenely down the aisle, her bright blue eyes connecting with Tyler's in a love-filled gaze.

Alexa slipped her hand into the crook of her father's elbow and they started down the aisle as the familiar strains of the wedding march filled the church.

Alexa saw her mother and brother, she saw Carrie and Tyler and the children, and a whole slew of Tremaines on one side of the church. On the other side, in the first pew was Kelsey and Gloria. Ron Cassidy, Ryan's father, sat beside them. At Ryan's request he had come alone, and there were no exes or steps present, again at Ryan's demand. He'd told Alexa he wanted no theatrics from any tenuous Cassidy connection. He wanted their wedding day to be wonderfully memorable, not notoriously so.

Ryan stood at the altar, tall and handsome, his dark eyes adoring his bride as she walked toward him. Though he'd been impatient to marry her and raring to begin living with her, now that the seven month courtship was over, he had to agree it had been a wise idea. He and Alexa had enjoyed each other, relearning things about each other and discovering new things, strengthening the bonds between them without the games, stress and uncertainty that had hampered them the first time around.

He had worked hard to win back Carrie's and Ben's goodwill because he knew how important her sister and brother were to Alexa. The already-strong ties between them were deepened as they put the unhappy past behind them, once and for all.

Alexa had continued her therapy with Kelsey; she knew and understood his daughter well, and Ryan was delighted at the warmth between them. And with Alexa in the picture, his dealings with Melissa had improved, mainly because he let Alexa deal with Melissa. It continued to be a source of amazement to him that Alexa found Melissa reasonable, and Melissa did not subject Alexa to her irritating bouts of histrionics.

Alexa and her father reached the altar, and the colonel handed his daughter over to her future husband. Ryan and Alexa smiled at each other, their eyes silently communicating the devotion and commitment they were about to openly express in front of their family and friends.

Ryan reached over and took her hand in his. "This is the happiest day of my life," he murmured to Alexa.

"And there are going to be so very many more," she promised him.

* * * * *

Silhouette Desire

COMING NEXT MONTH

ANOTHER TIME, ANOTHER PLACE
BJ James

When he saw Jennifer Burke once more, Mac McLachlan realized that ten years had not washed her out of his system. But, as they were still married, perhaps they could salvage something?

FEATHERS AND LACE
Karen Leabo

Financial whizz Zach Shaner inherited a floundering ostrich farm with a *very* enthusiastic manager. Ellie Kessler wanted Zach to fall in love with the ranch, the birds *and her*!

PLAYING WITH FIRE
Mary Maxwell

Carly Bradford understood that pilot Reece Cameron was desperate to find his son. Her niece Megan had recently become the focus of her world, although Carly knew that Megan would be happy to expand their little family to include Reece if only he would take the love that was on offer...

Silhouette Desire

COMING NEXT MONTH

FORTUNE'S COOKIE
Nancy Martin

Hard-nosed reporter Nick Fortune wasn't thrilled to be
asked to 'baby-sit' his boss's high-society niece. But Lorna
Kincaid had something to prove and was determined to
show the sexy chauvinist just how talented she was!

UNLIKELY EDEN
Anne Marie Winston

Meredith Bayliss was hoping to find a living, breathing
remnant of the dinosaur age during her rain forest
expedition—and Jared Adamson was certainly a candidate!
He was big, tough and keen to chase her through the jungle.

TUMBLEWEED AND GIBRALTAR
Rita Rainville

Finally free of responsibility, Stacy Sullivan was travelling
and seeking adventure. But when her car broke down on
Mac McClain's ranch, he ignored all her protests and took
charge. She was staying put for the foreseeable...

COMING NEXT MONTH FROM
Silhouette

Sensation
romance with a special mix of adventure,
glamour and drama

RACE AGAINST TIME Justine Davis
BAD MOON RISING Kathleen Eagle
MEMORIES OF LAURA Marilyn Pappano
STRANGERS IN PARADISE Heather Graham Pozzessere

Special Edition

longer, satisfying romances with
mature heroines and lots of emotion

POINT OF DEPARTURE Lindsay McKenna
FOREVER Ginna Gray
A DARING VOW Sherryl Woods
THE MAGIC OF CHRISTMAS Andrea Edwards
MAGNOLIA DAWN Erica Spindler
SINGLE MOTHER Jean Ann Donathan

DIAL 'D' FOR DESIRE
Win a year's supply of 'Silhouette Desires'
ABSOLUTELY FREE?

Yes, you can win one whole year's supply of 'Silhouette Desires'. It's easy! All you have to do is convert the four sets of numbers below into television soaps by using the letters in the telephone dial. Fill in your answers plus your name and address details overleaf, cut out and send to us by 31st October 1994.

1 5233315767 _____

2 3552 152 1819 _____

3 165547322 _____

4 2177252267 _____

Please turn over for entry details

DIAL 'D' FOR DESIRE
SEND YOUR ENTRY NOW!

The first five correct entries picked out of the bag after the closing date will each win one year's supply of 'Silhouette Desires' (six books every month - worth over £85). What could be easier?

Don't forget to enter your name and address in the space below then put this page in an envelope and post it today (you don't need a stamp). Competition closes 31st October 1994.

> **DIAL 'D' FOR DESIRE Competition**
> **FREEPOST**
> **P.O. Box 236**
> **Croydon**
> **Surrey CR9 9EL**

COMSD

Are you a Reader Service subscriber?   Yes ☐   No ☐

Ms/Mrs/Miss/Mr _____

Address _____

_____

_____

Postcode _____

Signature _____

One application per household. Offer valid only in U.K. and Eire. You may be mailed with offers from other reputable companies as a result of this application. Please tick box if you would prefer not to receive such offers. ☐